Valley of the
Wandering River

Valley of the Wandering River

A Western Duo

Ray Hogan

Five Star • Waterville, Maine

First Edition
First Printing: March 2003

Published in 2003 in conjunction with
Golden West Literary Agency.

Set in 11 pt. Plantin by Myrna S. Raven.

Printed in the United States on permanent paper.

Library of Congress Cataloging-in-Publication Data

Hogan, Ray, 1908–
    [Track the man down]
    Valley of the wandering river : a western duo /
by Ray Hogan.
        p. cm.
    Contents: Track the man down—Valley of the wandering
river.
    ISBN 0-7862-3773-2 (hc : alk. paper)
    1. Western stories.   I. Hogan, Ray, 1908– Valley of the
wandering river.   II. Title.
PS3558.O3473 T68 2003
    813'.54—dc21   2002068974

Valley of the Wandering River

TABLE OF CONTENTS

Track the Man Down

I

The road south, out of Santa Fé, had been long and tiresome. Ben Dunn, slouched in the corner seat of the stagecoach, let his body roll and toss with the swaying, pitching vehicle and stared across the vast carpet that was New Mexico Territory. In one more hour they would reach Crawford's Crossing. There he would quit the groaning Concord, pick up his horse, and begin the final twenty mile trip home.

The coach veered suddenly, reeled to one side as it plunged into an arroyo. Dust puffs exploded from the corners behind the seats, and the vehicle cracked and popped loudly. Outside, on the box, the driver shrilled his curses, fought with the leather ribbons laced between his fingers.

"Git on there, Brownie! *Hi-eeee-ah!* Blaze! Git along, you jugheaded broomtails!"

The coach righted itself, snapped back into line as the four-up lunged into the harness, took up the slack. Dunn, displaced from his corner by the lurching motion, readjusted himself. He was glad the long journey to the capital, in Santa Fé, was about over.

It seemed like he had been riding for weeks instead of days, and he would never have made the trip had there been any choice. But the matter of the dispute that lay between himself and Isaac Pope, whose quarter million acres of Diamond X Ranch lay west of his, had to be settled. Pope was dying, and, if the problem waited, there would never be any straightening it out with Jack Marr who would inherit the spread once the crusty, old rancher was gone. It would be settled now. The small cañon that ran between them—the bone of contention—was clearly on his Box B property. The spring from which flowed a steady stream of clear, sweet water was his. He had with him a certified map from the Land Office to prove it. Once Isaac Pope saw the map, it would be ended; for, despite his rapacious nature, Pope was a fair man. He would claim nothing that was not rightfully his.

Dunn was glad the quarrel was soon to end. The peace and contentment he had found on the Comanche Flats, these past three years, had afforded him a way of life far different from the precarious and wary existence he had endured before going there. He did not want it to end. When he purchased and moved onto the small, rag-tag ranch he renamed the Box B, he had been quite alone on the flats. There were only two other inhabitants within reasonable distance—Abner and Hopeful Loveless, an elderly couple who lived in a shack at the foot of Comanche Mountain. They actually were within Dunn's property, but he permitted them to live on the small plot of ground they had chosen and eke out a livelihood from the soil.

After a time he hired Loveless during periods when he needed help, usually the spring and summer months. Dunn's herd was small, never over a couple of hundred steers, and he had a half dozen horses. He intentionally kept it that way. He had little use for money since his needs were few. Once a year he sold off twenty or thirty head of beef and that provided him with enough hard money to purchase necessities and pay Abner Loveless for what services he had rendered.

He had seen little of Pope and his right-hand man, Jack Marr, who, Abner once told him, was no real kin. Pope had no family of his own and had taken in Marr to raise as a son. Together they had built up the Diamond X to become the largest and most respected ranch in that part of the territory. They had left Ben Dunn alone, and all had gone well until the change took place. With it had come the dispute over the spring. Pope decided to move his ranch buildings off the flats, to a new, more desirable position at the foot of Comanche Mountain. Trouble had come swiftly—sharp words with Marr, several clashes with Diamond X riders. An attempt to reason with old Isaac got him nowhere. It had all resulted in the hurried trip to Santa Fé for a copy of the Land Office map.

"*Hi-eee-ah,* Brownie! Spot! Blaze! Satan! Git along! Git along!"

Dunn glanced out the window. He was the only passenger, and now he moved across to the opposite seat in order that he might better see. The country was taking on a more familiar look. They were drawing nearer to Crawford's Crossing. He recognized the low run of red-faced bluffs to the south, and the lengthy, flat-lying ridge that paralleled the road that led to his ranch. He straightened up and stretched his wide shoulders. It wouldn't be too long now.

It was mid-morning when they pulled to a halt before the squat, adobe buildings where Tom Crawford operated a combination stage stop, general store, and livery stable. It was no regular breaking point in the line's schedule, so there was no horse change. It was merely a pause in the long run to El Paso.

Dunn swung down from the coach, waited while the driver dug out his valise from the iron-railed baggage area behind the box. He caught the bag when it dropped, turned away. From the gallery that fronted the store, Crawford greeted him.

" 'Mornin', Ben. Glad you're back."

Dunn stepped up onto the porch, followed the man into the store. He said: "Any particular reason?"

"Could be," the storekeeper answered. "Sabine and Pete Frisco were by here early today. Way they were talkin', somethin' must have happened over at your place."

Dunn stiffened as alarm moved quickly through him. Bibo Sabine and Pete Frisco worked for Pope—or, rather, for Jack Marr. Both men were hardcases, accustomed more to using a gun than a rope.

"Any idea what it was? They say anything about Abner?"

Crawford scratched his stubbled chin. He shook his head. "Nope. But I gathered they gave him a rough time over that spring you and Pope are bickerin' about. You get that proof you went after?"

Dunn patted his inside pocket. "Right here," he said. He moved to the front of the store, threw his glance across the way to Finley's Saloon. If the two Diamond X men were still around, they would be found there. There were no horses at the rail. The stage driver, having tarried long enough to quench his thirst, was just coming through the doorway.

"They didn't hang around long," Crawford said, reading his mind. "Headed back for Pope's after they got themselves a few snorts."

Dunn said: "I see. My horse ready?"

"Waitin' in the stable," Crawford answered. "When I heard the stage comin', I told Manuel to saddle him up. Figured you'd be in a hurry."

"Obliged," Dunn said, and reached for the door handle.

"That wire and other stuff you ordered got in," the storekeeper said then. "You want to take it now? You're welcome to use my wagon."

14

Dunn said: "No time. Better get to the ranch and see if Abner's all right. I'll drive in tomorrow and pick it up."

"Good enough. It'll be ready to load."

His bay horse was waiting for him when he circled Crawford's building and entered the low-roofed stable, a hundred feet or so to its rear. He gave his thanks to the Mexican hostler and swung into the saddle. Anger and worry hammered through him in a steady throb, and he lost no time covering the score of miles that lay between his Box B Ranch and the stage stop.

A feeling of relief coursed through him as he rode down the last slope. His small house with its scatter of outbuildings still stood in the clearing. They had not been damaged or burned, as he had feared. Now, if Abner was all right. . . .

The old rider came from the barn at that moment. He limped noticeably and the left side of his veined face was swollen. He halted in front of the wide doors, lifted his hand in greeting.

" 'Afternoon, son. See you made it."

Relief flowed through Dunn. Loveless was not badly injured, but the anger within the rancher did not lessen. He dismounted, looked at the older man closely. "This come of Sabine's work?"

Loveless said: "What? Oh, you mean this here jaw of mine. Yeah, Bibo sort of pushed me around some. Not bad. I been slapped around before, and lots worse than this."

"Bibo's a big man," Dunn commented, sarcasm heavy in his voice. "What was it all about . . . the spring?"

"The same," Abner replied. "Saw your waterin' pond gettin' low. Rode up to see what the trouble was. Pope's bunch had dammed up our ditch and dug a new one that

15

ran to their side of the hill. Was changin' it back when Bibo and Pete Frisco come along."

The simmering anger within Ben Dunn exploded in an oath. "I'm going to straighten this out with Pope, once and for all! You get home all right?"

"Sure," Loveless said. "You ridin' over to see him right now?"

"Right now," Dunn echoed. "Got the proof I need to convince him that the spring is on my land. I'll let him look it over, then tomorrow we'll fence off the cañon. Be no more of this. I was willing to share the water with Pope, but now he and his Diamond X bunch can go hang!"

"Spring ain't big enough to share, anyway," Loveless observed.

"Big enough if they didn't try to hog it," Dunn said. He moved back to his horse, stepped to the saddle. "You go on home. When I get ready to start stringing that fence, I'll come for you."

Loveless said: "Good enough. Now, watch yourself at Pope's. Like walkin' around in a nest of rattlesnakes."

Dunn favored the old man with a wry grin. "If we're goin' to keep on living around here, I guess this is the time to start pulling some fangs."

"That's for damned sure!" Abner Loveless said. "Good luck to you!"

It was near supper hour when Dunn rode into the wide, hard-packed yard of Pope's Diamond X Ranch and halted before the main house. He dismounted, looped the reins of the bay about the hitch rail. He wheeled slowly, let his eyes sweep over the buildings of the ranch. All were good, well-built structures, and in excellent repair. Pope had a fine place. He stepped up onto the gallery, made his way to the door, and knocked.

It opened almost immediately. Evidently Jack Marr had been standing just inside for some time. He was a tall man, probably twenty-five years old, which made him about the same age as Dunn. He had dark eyes and hair, a narrow face accented somewhat by hollow cheeks. His mouth was small, his teeth too fine and white. Those things, linked with a thin, aquiline nose, destroyed any claim to handsomeness and bestowed, instead, a definite cunning to his countenance. He regarded Ben with surly suspicion.

"What's on your mind, Dunn?"

"Little matter I mean to take up with Pope," Ben answered, and stepped by Marr. He entered a large room, cluttered with heavy, leather-covered furniture, a huge oak table with lion's-paw legs. There were mounted game heads on the walls and tanned skins upon the floor.

"I look after things here," Marr said coldly. "Take it up with me."

Dunn shook his head. "No, I came to see Pope. Either lead me to him or I'll find him myself."

Marr studied Dunn's set jaw for a brief time. Then he said: "All right. Follow me."

He started toward the back of the house, the polish on his blood-colored, handmade boots glowing dully in the subdued light. Marr wore the best when it came to clothing. His broadcloth suits cost more than most cowboys made in three months of hard work, Ben guessed.

"In here," Marr said in his flat voice.

They had reached an open door at the end of the hall. Inside the room Ben saw Isaac Pope lying on a bed. His first glance at the rancher showed him that the man, indeed, was in a bad way. His skin was like old paper, yellowed and cracked. He was little more than a skeleton with lusterless eyes sunken deeply into his skull. He had changed greatly since their last meeting at the disputed spring. At that time Pope had been well enough to sit in a saddle and snarl his orders. Now it appeared doubtful that he could even raise his head.

"Who's there? What do you want?"

Pope's question was a dry, impatient crackle of words. Ben moved beside the bed. He drew the Land Office map he had obtained in Santa Fé from his pocket.

"It's Dunn," he said, answering the old rancher. "I've come about that spring you claimed was on your land. I brought a map to show you that it's not. It belongs to me."

Isaac Pope fastened his baleful glare upon Ben. "Map? What kind of map?"

"One the Land Office made up. Shows your exact property lines. That spring's on my side, just like I told you."

The rancher struggled to a sitting position. He extended his gnarled hand for the paper. "Show me," he ordered. "You show me where the line is."

Dunn held the map before him, indicated the area in question with a forefinger. He traced the boundaries of the two ranches. Pope studied them for several minutes. Apparently satisfied on that score, he examined the official markings on the stiff paper, assuring himself of the map's authenticity.

"Reckon you're right, Dunn," he said, and sank back onto his pillow. "Look at it, Jack, so's you'll know."

Marr stepped in closer. He scarcely glanced at the map. "I see it," he said.

"That settles it," Pope stated, releasing his grasp of the paper. "It's on your property, Dunn. I'll make no more claim to it. And you forget about it, Jack. Tell the rest of the crew to do the same."

Marr said: "Sure, Pa. Not much good to us, anyway."

"Water's always a good thing in this country," Pope crackled. "But that ain't none of ours, so forget it."

"Sure, Pa," Marr said.

Dunn refolded the map, thrust it into his pocket. He started to say something to Pope about the state of his health, to express a hope that he would be better soon. But he changed his mind. Isaac Pope was not the sort of man to whom you conveyed such sentiments. Instead, he said: "I'll be going, Mister Pope. Glad we got this ironed out with no big trouble."

The rancher threshed about beneath the thin coverlet. "All right! All right! I said it was yours. Now get out of here and let me rest!"

Dunn wheeled and returned to the hall. Marr followed. When they reached the front room, Marr reached out, laid his hand on Ben's arm.

"I expect to keep on using water from that spring, Dunn. Don't go doing anything foolish, like fencing it off."

Dunn knocked Marr's hand aside. "There will be wire across that cañon soon as I can string it," he stated. "Don't want to see you or any Diamond X rider, or any of your stock on my side again. That clear?"

Marr's thin face was expressionless. "Don't put up any fences, Dunn. This is the only warning I'm going to give you!"

II

Ben Dunn was in Crawford's Crossing early the next morning. Well before daybreak, he had harnessed up his team of bays to the light spring wagon and made the trip to the supply point. Crawford had expected him. He had the supplies out on the gallery, waiting to be loaded.

"Anything serious happen yesterday?" the merchant asked as he helped Dunn stow the boxes of groceries and spools of wire in the vehicle. "Abner get hurt bad?"

Dunn said: "Sabine roughed him up a mite. Little matter I've got to take up with Bibo, first time I run across him."

"Could be right soon," Crawford said. "He and Pete Frisco rode in a couple hours ago. They're over in Finley's Saloon now, easin' their thirst. You get squared around with old Isaac?"

Dunn nodded. "We had an understanding," he said noncommittally. He shoved the last box of supplies into a corner of the wagon bed, drew a light tarp over it all to keep out the dust.

From down the road came the sound of running horses, the clatter of metal and cracking of wood. Crawford drew a thick, silver watch from his vest pocket, squinted at its face.

"Stage's right on time," he said.

Dunn grunted, straightened up. He threw his glance across the way to the saloon. "All of a sudden I've got me a thirst," he said. "Think I'll pay Finley a visit."

Crawford eyed the rancher speculatively. "You right sure it's a drink you're lookin' for?"

Dunn grinned. "Man never knows who he's going to run

into in a saloon," he said, and stepped off the porch.

The stage whirled into the yard in a boiling cloud of dust. It skidded to a halt. The driver wrapped the reins around the whip stock, swung down. Dunn paused, watching him turn to the door and open it.

"Crawford's Crossing, miss. This is the place."

A flamboyantly dressed girl of seventeen, or possibly eighteen, appeared. She was not particularly pretty, but she had clear, blue eyes, dark hair, and thick, equally dark brows. Her mouth was wide, with generous lips. The soft creaminess of her skin was proof she was no permanent inhabitant of the frontier.

The driver assisted the girl to alight. He looked at her closely. "Miss, you sure this is the place where you want off? Ain't nothin' here but that store and that saloon, over there."

Her face was pale. "I thought it would be a town."

"No town closer than a hundred miles. You want to go on?"

Ben Dunn watched the girl, waited for her to answer. He was having a difficult time getting her classified in his mind. The dress she wore was a bit garish and bold. It was cut far too low at the neckline, much too short at the hem. Yet her face belied the thought. There was none of the customary commonness to her. There was no harshness to her features, no hardness in her eyes. It was as though she were dressed in another's garments—an angel in the cloak of a fancy woman.

"No, I'll have to stay," the girl said firmly. She took her small carpetbag from him, tucked it under an arm.

Sabine and Frisco, unaware of Dunn's presence on the far side of the coach, strolled into the yard from the saloon.

"What you bringin' us, Harry?" Sabine called to the driver.

21

"Lady bought a ticket to here," the man replied. "All I know about it." He centered his attention on the girl once more. "You sure you don't want to go on, miss?"

She drew her light cloth stole more closely about her shoulders. "No, this is where I want off."

"Go on, Harry," Sabine said. "Lady's made up her mind to stay, and I'm sure goin' to make her welcome."

The stage driver climbed back onto his perch. He unwound the leather ribbons, glanced at Crawford. "You got anything for me, Tom?"

"Nothin'," Crawford answered.

The driver shouted at his horses, and the stage lurched and plunged out of the yard. The girl watched it leave, and then turned to Crawford, a look of helplessness on her face.

Bibo Sabine said: "Right this way, girlie. The saloon's over here." He swaggered to her side, took her by the arm.

Dunn saw horror and fear spring into her eyes. He stepped away from his team, moved swiftly up to Sabine. He drove a rock-hard fist into Sabine's jaw. The Diamond X rider yelled, went backward, and sprawled in the dust.

"Get up!" Dunn said. "Got a couple of things to settle with you."

Sabine scrambled to his feet. He glared at Dunn, his thick shoulders hunched forward, arms akimbo. A low mutter of curses trickled from his thick lips.

"Looked for you yesterday at Pope's," Dunn said. "Seems you wanna slap old men around. Like Abner Loveless. How about trying it on me?"

Sabine said nothing, simply lunged. Dunn stepped lightly to one side. As Sabine went by, he smashed him to the ground with a down-sledging right. The cowboy came up fast, whirled. Dunn doubled him over with a sharp left to the belly, straightened him up with a right to the chin. Sabine gasped, staggered back.

"This one's for Abner," Dunn said, and sent a straight right to the cowboy's nose.

Sabine went down hard. From the edge of his eye, Ben Dunn saw Frisco move in on the right. He wheeled to face the man. His heavy six-gun came magically into his hand. Pete Frisco halted.

"You name it," Dunn said softly.

Frisco waited out a long minute. He shook his head. "Reckon it ain't for me."

Dunn said: "All right. Load up Sabine and get out of here."

Frisco crossed over, helped the dazed Sabine to his horse. Dunn waited until they had ridden from the yard, and then turned to the girl. The anger within him had dwindled, but there was still a faint edge to his voice.

"Somebody supposed to meet you here?"

She said: "No. Nobody knew I was coming. Can you tell me where the Pope ranch is?"

Dunn stared at her.

From the porch Crawford said: "About thirty-five miles due west. You goin' to walk?"

The girl did not smile at the weak jest. "I didn't think it was so far. Isn't there a stagecoach?"

"Not going in that direction," Dunn said. "You sure it's the Pope place you want?"

"Yes, Isaac Pope."

Dunn said: "Well, my place is about fifteen miles this side. If you're willing to ride in my wagon, I'll take you there."

Relief showed in her face. "Thank you," she murmured. "I'll be ever so grateful, Mister . . . ?"

"Ben Dunn," he supplied, and handed her up to the wagon seat.

"Mister Dunn," she finished. "My name is Laura. Laura Pope. I'm Isaac Pope's daughter."

Dunn froze where he stood, staring at the girl in astonishment. Crawford, leaning against the door frame of his building, snorted. "Buzzards are already beginnin' to gather."

Dunn flung a sharp glance at the storekeeper. "Never mind, Tom," he said. He circled the wagon, climbed up onto the seat beside the girl. He gathered up the reins, slapped the horses on their broad backs. They leaped forward, and the vehicle rolled out of the yard, settled into the ruts that struck into the west.

After a few minutes, she said: "You don't believe me, do you? About being Isaac Pope's daughter, I mean."

Dunn was busy with the horses. After a brief time he answered her. "Who am I to question it? You say you are. As far as I'm concerned, you are. Guess you caught me by surprise with it."

"But I *am* Laura Pope! Is it so strange that he should have a daughter?"

The bays felt good and were fighting him, anxious to run. Dunn gave in, letting them have their way. The road across the flat plain was fairly good. Later, when they drew nearer the mountain, he would have to slow them down, make them take it easy.

He said: "Always heard Pope had no family. Reason he took in Jack Marr."

"Jack Marr? Who is he?"

"The son of some friend of Pope's. Brought him into his house when he was a kid. Raised him like he was his own son."

The girl considered that. "I see. What did that man back at the store mean . . . about the buzzards gathering?"

His eyes on the road, Dunn explained. "Pope's dying. Probably won't be long now. His place is worth a lot of money. Crawford meant there probably would be a lot of people showing up, wanting to get their fingers in the pie."

"I didn't know he was sick," Laura said wearily. "But that's the way it would be. It's only what I should expect."

He glanced at her, noted the hopelessness in her eyes. "Meaning what?"

"After sixteen years I finally learn who my real father is, only to find him dying, maybe already dead."

A covey of blue-feathered quail suddenly whirred off from beneath the horses' hoofs. The team shied violently, carrying the wagon out of the road in a wild detour. Dunn went forward in the seat. Crouched like a Roman chariot driver, he got them back into the shallow ruts. The sun was climbing higher in its clean, cloudless arch, and it had turned increasingly warmer. When the bays were again in line, sweat stood out on Dunn's brow in large beads. He brushed it away with a sweep of his hand.

"Lot of people going to think like Crawford," he said. "Be natural, with you showing up right at this time . . . and wearing clothes like you have on."

She looked down at her dress. "The only ones I had, and they were my mother's."

"Your mother's?" he repeated, frowning.

"Yes. She died about six months ago."

"Sorry to hear it," he mumbled.

The team was running free down a long, gentle grade. He wrapped the reins around the ship, removed his leather jacket, and tossed it into the rear of the wagon. He looked ahead, searched his memory and the land for a suitable place to halt for lunch. There was a shallow arroyo, he recalled, a few miles on. It offered a scatter of thin cottonwood trees, but no water. Still, it would be better than open ground.

"Expect you're hungry," he said. "We'll pull up and eat soon."

She made no reply, simply stared out over the plain. He glanced at her, wondering if she had heard.

"This country is so big . . . so lonely," she said, almost to herself. "It's filled with emptiness."

Dunn laughed. "Reckon that's about as near right as you could say it. But you get used to it. Once you know it, you'll never like any other place."

"Have you lived here long?"

"Around here since the war."

"The war," she repeated in a falling voice. "It changed so much for all of us."

They reached the cottonwoods shortly after that, and halted. Dunn picketed the team on a small stand of short grass, turned to prepare lunch. From his saddlebags under the wagon's seat, he obtained a blackened coffee pot and a sack of dark coffee beans. He crushed a handful between two rocks, dumped the grains into the container. He added water from the canteen and set it over a quick fire. While it came to a boil, he got the crackers, some tinned meat, and a can of peaches from the groceries Crawford had furnished him.

"Not much of a feed," he said to the girl when it was ready. "Reckon it will do until we reach my place."

She ate in silence, and, when they were finished, she went quietly about cleaning up and restoring the provisions and equipment to their customary containers. That done, she turned and looked at Ben Dunn with grave eyes.

26

"Is this dress really so bad?" she asked, as if she had been thinking about what he had said. "I thought it was pretty."

"It is," he agreed, "but hardly what a man would expect his daughter to be seen in."

"I had nothing else to wear," she said, sitting down beside him. "I want you to know that. The way I may look now has nothing to do with what I am."

"I could see that," Dunn said. "But other men will think different. . . ."

She said: "I know. There were a few times on the trip out here. . . ."

"People have a way of judging others by their appearance. Generally wrong."

"True, but I would like you to know the story. I want you to understand."

"It's all right," he said. "If it hurts to talk about it, let it ride."

"But I want you to hear it. You should have the straight of it. You're the only friend I've had since I left home. You're entitled to the truth."

He said no more. He fished a match from his shirt pocket, struck it. He held the small flame to the tip of his cigarette, inhaled deeply. The sound of the horses cropping at grass was a steady crunch on the still air. High overhead a Mexican eagle soared in lazy circles.

"I never knew my father, my real father, I mean. I was born here, on his ranch, but when I was about two years old, my mother took me and ran off with a drummer. She couldn't stand the terrible loneliness of this country. She was a Saint Louis girl and not used to the sort of life Isaac Pope offered her."

Laura paused, glanced at Dunn. He was watching the

27

gliding eagle, cigarette drooping from one corner of his lips.

"I don't recall much until I was six or seven. I do remember that we traveled around a lot, went from town to town. I thought Corey Phillips was my father. Everybody always called my mother Missus Phillips. I know now they were never married because she and Mister Pope were never divorced. We were all happy, and then the war came along. Corey was killed in one of the very first battles. Things just sort of went to pieces for us after that, and we finally ended up in a mining town in Pennsylvania where mother took a job in a saloon. I guess I knew it wasn't a very nice job, and she knew it, too. But we had to live and eat, and there weren't any jobs for women, especially after the war was over. My mother never let me see where she worked, but I knew about it. I stayed at home, kept house, and went to school. I used to make fifty cents a week looking after the babies that belonged to two of the women who worked with my mother. It wasn't much, but it helped a little. Mother never was able to bring home much money."

"She must have been a fine woman," Dunn said. "Takes a lot of courage to keep on going, like she did."

Laura gave him a grateful smile. "About a year ago she took sick. She got to where she couldn't go to work, and we had to depend on the charity of friends. She grew worse, and we both realized she was going to die."

The girl halted abruptly, looked away. Dunn said—"You don't have to go on."—in a kindly voice.

She sat up straighter. "I want to!" she said. She waited several moments, then continued. "That was when I found out about my real father, Isaac Pope. Mother told me the whole story, said I was to go to him after she passed on. She said he would never forgive her, but that he would hold nothing against me, his own daughter. She wrote a letter to him so he would know who I am. I have it here in my bag, along with a picture she gave me. Would you like to see them?"

Dunn shook his head. "They're for Pope, not me."

"After she was gone, I got ready to leave. There were only a few dollars, little else, but I sold what I could to raise the fare. Mother's friends all helped, donated what they could. I heard that someone passed a hat at the place where mother worked to take care of Molly's daughter, as they called me. I finally got enough together to buy a ticket. There wasn't anything left over for clothing, so I wore a dress of my mother's, along with some things her friends gave me. That's why I'm dressed as I am. I had no other choice.

"It has been a long ride from Pennsylvania, and I'm glad it's about over with. I'll see my father, tell him what mother told me, and show him the letter and picture. If he welcomes me, I will be thankful. If not, I'll just have to go on, find myself a job of some sort, somewhere. Maybe out here, in this new country, a girl can find a decent job. I don't want anything from my father except a home . . . and that only if he wants to give it willingly. If he doesn't . . . well, I'll manage some way."

Dunn glanced at her. "The kind of work you'll find in this country won't be much different from the kind your mother found in Pennsylvania."

"Then, if that's the answer, that's the way it will be. I can be as strong and as brave as my mother, if I have to. I don't want it that way, but I've already learned we don't get to have things the way we'd like."

Dunn reached over, laid his hand upon hers. "Maybe it will all work out for you," he said gently. "Don't worry too much about it. Isaac Pope is a hard man, but he's honest and he's fair. He'll do the right thing. I'm not very welcome around his place, but if there's anything I can do to help. . . ."

"Thank you," she murmured. "Just being my friend and listening to me is all I ask."

They packed up and moved out shortly after that. The afternoon wore on. They reached the bottomlands, as the area was generally called, rolled swiftly along a rocky, brush-lined road. Dunn's Box B spread was less than a mile distant now. It was almost full dark and night would be upon them by the time they arrived at his place. He was debating the best course to follow, whether to stop at his ranch, eat and rest for a time, or simply obtain fresh horses and continue on to Pope's. Laura was tired, he knew, but likely she was anxious to complete the journey.

He turned to her. "You feel up to riding fifteen miles more tonight? It will have to be on horseback. . . ."

A gunshot suddenly blasted through the dark hush. Off to their right and close at hand. Dunn grabbed for his gun, tried to hold in the bays. From a remote corner of his memory a single name rushed forward, exploded from his lips.

"Greavey!"

A wild yell followed the shot. The bays swerved sharply, nearly overturning the wagon. Dunn forgot his weapon, sawed at the reins as he tried to bring the frantic team back onto the road.

"Hold on!" he yelled as the wagon bounced and rocked over the uneven ground.

More shooting erupted. Dunn heard the shrill whine of bullets. The bays, thoroughly frightened now, plunged down the narrow alleyway between trees and shrubbery.

The wagon swayed dangerously, whipped back and forth like a string in a stiff breeze.

"Look out!"

Dunn shouted a warning. A large rock was suddenly in the road before them. He tried to swing the wagon to one side to avoid it. The left-side front wheel smashed into it, crumpled with a loud popping sound. The hub hit into the soft earth and hung momentarily. The vehicle left the ground and flipped over with a crash.

III

Ben Dunn struck on all four. Groceries and other supplies showered down around him like rain. One of the spools of wire came up against his leg, almost knocking him flat. He ignored it all, glanced wildly about for Laura. He saw her, a crumpled shape off to his right.

He got to his feet, raced to where she lay. The team, hampered now by the wagon's dead weight, had stopped a dozen yards down the road. He dropped to the girl's side, slipped his arm under her shoulders, and raised her carefully.

"Laura!" he said. "Laura!"

She opened her eyes slowly, stared up at him. "What happened . . . ?"

"Everything's all right now," he replied. "You got a tap on the head when the wagon went over. How do you feel?"

"A little dizzy," she said. "Are you hurt?"

He shook his head. "Was lucky." He raised his eyes, looked about. "Whoever it was, he's gone now. We're only a short way from my place. Rest here until I unhitch the team, then we'll go on. I'll pick up the pieces tomorrow," he added ruefully, surveying the scatter of items.

He left her, went to the heaving bays, and freed them. They were quiet now. He led them back to Laura. She was sitting up when he reached her. He could see she was badly shaken.

"Can you ride?" he asked, kneeling beside her.

She said: "I think so. I'll try."

He helped her onto one of the horses. She took a firm

32

grasp of the harness. "Who was it that caused the runaway? Do you know?"

"Didn't see anybody. But I've got a pretty good idea. Hold on. We don't have to go far."

He walked ahead of the horses, led them down the road through the darkness. He was thinking of how strange it was that Jay Greavey, an enemy of the past, should have come into his mind when the ambush exploded about them. Likely it had been Bibo Sabine and Pete Frisco, endeavoring to get even for the incident at Crawford's Crossing.

They reached the Box B, entered the yard. He halted the bays in front of his small, three-room house, and turned to Laura. He reached out, took her under the arms, and swung her to the ground.

"Wait here. I'll go inside and light a lamp."

He went immediately to the door, pushed it back, and entered. The room filled with a warm, cheery glow. He wheeled to call Laura, found her standing in the doorway, watching him.

"You can use that room there," he said, and pointed to his own sleeping quarters. "Soon as I look after the horses, I'll fix a bite to eat."

The girl did not move. "I didn't expect to stay the night."

He saw the uncertainty in her eyes. "I don't think you're in any condition to make the ride. It's a hard fifteen miles."

He crossed the room, threw open the door that led into the bedroom. "You'll be safe. You can lock the door, if you like. I'll lay myself a pallet on the kitchen floor."

"I won't be afraid," she said, and stepped by him.

He went into the yard, took the bays into the barn. He removed their harness, and they walked into their customary stalls. He threw down some feed for them, and came back into the open. Suddenly deciding he should do something about the groceries he had left strewn around the wrecked wagon, he took his wheelbarrow and returned to where the mishap had occurred. He loaded up all things that might draw wild animals during the night, added to them Laura's valise and his saddlebags, and went back to the house.

When he entered, he was pleasantly surprised to see that she had taken over. She had built a fire in the stove. On it coffee was already beginning to boil, and the frying pan was popping with hot grease. She half turned when he came in, smiled at him.

"Felt I should do something," she said. "Hope you don't mind. Will meat and potatoes be all right? And cornmeal muffins?"

"Sounds good to me," Dunn replied. "You feel up to it?"

"Certainly," she said, and resumed her work. "Are you finished outside?"

"All done. And I brought your bag."

He finished stowing away the supplies on the shelf. The room was beginning to fill with tantalizing odors of frying meat and potatoes, the rich flavor of coffee. He pulled back a chair, seated himself at the table. Without asking, she poured him a cupful of the steaming black liquid.

"Food won't be long," she said.

He found himself enjoying the moments, the easy relaxation. He watched her, busy at work. He listened as she lightly hummed the words of an old war tune. He found himself thinking—*This is the way a man should live.*—and wished it might be so for him.

"Don't you get lonely here, living all by yourself?" she asked suddenly.

He thought for a moment. "Maybe so. Never gave it much notice till now. When you're busy and got a lot of work to do, it just never occurs to you. Right now, however, I'm seeing how much I've missed."

She smiled at him. "I take that as a nice compliment, Mister Dunn," she said. "Thank you. I guess we're ready to eat."

Both hungry, they ate in silence. To Ben Dunn the meal was delicious, surpassing by far any he had eaten in the restaurants along the trails, or that he had prepared for himself. He had fried meat and potatoes innumerable times, but never had they had the savory qualities of these. It was the woman's touch, he decided.

He told her so, and added: "Leave the dishes. I'll take care of them tomorrow. You ought to rest. That was a bad knock you got on the head."

"I'm all right," she said. "Besides, we'll need them for breakfast. Drink your coffee. I made plenty. It will take me just a few minutes to clean up."

Dunn produced his old pipe, tamped it full of rough-cut tobacco. He lit it, settled back. A man never realized what he was missing—until he had a sample of what genuine living was.

The faint scrape of leather outside in the yard cut through his thoughts. It brought him to his feet instantly. In one swift motion he killed the light in the lamp, whirled to the door.

"Greavey!"

The name again unconsciously blurted from his lips. He dropped to a crouch, opened the latch. He jerked the door wide, plunged into the night, gun ready in his hand. There was no one there. The yard was empty. Then he heard, faintly, the hollow, retreating hoof beats of a running horse.

Whoever it had been was gone.

He wheeled slowly, returned to the house. Sweat had gathered on his forehead and tension still showed in the hardness of his gray eyes. There was a measure of wonder in them, also, wonder as to why Jay Greavey was on his mind. Was the gunman somewhere near? Was intuition, somehow, voicing a warning within him?

Laura waited solemnly for him to turn up the lamp, resume his chair. She refilled his cup. The dishes were unfinished. She ignored them.

"Too late to see who it was," he murmured.

She sat down opposite him. "Who is Greavey? Twice I heard you mention his name, like he was someone you perhaps feared."

Dunn stirred. His brow clouded. "I don't think I'm afraid of him. It's just the waiting, I suppose, expecting him to come someday and have it out."

Horror spread through her eyes. "He wants to kill you? Why?"

He did not immediately answer. He studied his pipe moodily. Then: "I gunned down his brother, Tom. I went after him to take him on a murder charge. He decided to fight."

"And now he's looking for you. Were you a lawman of some sort?"

"In a way. Out here they call them bounty hunters. Not exactly a kindly name. I went after the outlaws the regular lawmen left alone. For the reward."

"Did you always have to kill them?"

He shook his head. "They had a choice. There were some who came along with no trouble, but not many. Because they are desperate men, they usually choose to fight rather than surrender and face a hangman's rope. You hear talk about bounty hunters being bloodthirsty killers. It's not exactly the truth. An outlaw picks his own way to go. I didn't want to kill Tom Greavey. He forced my hand. And when it was all over and I looked down at him and saw he was just a kid, something happened inside me. He could have been my own younger brother. It made me a little sick, and I quit bounty hunting right then. I'd saved up a little money and started looking for a place where I could settle down and work the land, raise some cattle. Guess I figured that by doing so, I could get it out of my system."

Dunn paused. His pipe had gone out, and he lit it again. "It worked pretty well . . . except you don't ever forget the things that have happened. The past is always there, no matter how hard you try to put it out of your mind. Someday Jay Greavey will come along, and we'll settle our score. And when he does, it will be finished, one way or another."

She shuddered at his words. They had shocked her. He realized that as he sat there. "Don't let it bother you," he said. "It's the way of things out here. A man picks his road to travel and stays with it, come hell or high wind. He's got nobody to blame but himself for the reckoning he someday has to make."

"But it's all so cold, so inhuman! To just sit and talk about killing, or being killed. Back East. . . ."

"Back East is a different world," he said, "and people there have no real idea of what it takes to stay alive in this country. Now, you had better get some rest. We've got a hard trip ahead of us in the morning, and it won't be on the seat of a wagon."

IV

Despite an early start, it was nearly ten o'clock the next morning when Laura and Dunn rode into Pope's Diamond X Ranch headquarters. Ben had offered her a pair of his old, faded denims in the interest of comfort, but since they were several sizes too large, she had declined.

Several of Pope's hired hands strolled out into the yard as they drew up to the hitching rail that fronted the main house, but none came forward to meet them. Dunn dismounted, helped Laura to do likewise.

She glanced around uncertainly. He could see she was uncertain, almost fearful of what lay ahead. He smiled at her. "Everything will be all right."

Her chin became firm. She thanked him with her eyes for his encouragement. "I ought to freshen up a bit before I see him. Where would I go to wash up and get the dust off?"

Dunn pointed to a door farther along the side of the building. "That's the kitchen. Pope has a Mexican woman cook. Why don't you see her?"

Laura said—"Thank you."—and turned away. Abruptly she halted. "And thank you for bringing me here, and everything else. I hope I haven't caused you too much trouble."

"Forget it," he said. "Was my pleasure. Good luck."

She continued on toward the rear of the house. Beyond her, in the yard, Dunn saw Bibo Sabine and several Diamond X cowpunchers give her their undivided attention. Sabine, a thin-faced, dark-eyed gunman of sorts who generally hung close to Marr, said something. They all laughed.

Dunn felt anger rise within him. He strode swiftly across the open ground, hauled up before the cowboy. Sabine's grin had died when he saw Dunn coming. He glanced about at the men beside him, his face now sullen and stiff.

Dunn said: "Appears I didn't make things clear enough at Crawford's yesterday."

He stepped forward, drove his fist into Sabine's jaw. The gunman staggered back, came up against the man directly behind him. Both went down in a tangle of legs and arms.

"Damn you!" Sabine yelled. "I'm gettin' tired of you. . . ."

Dunn's pistol came into his hand with a swift, fluid motion. The cowboys back of Sabine froze. The gunman scrambled to his feet. Anger distorted his face, turned it a beet red.

"Who you think you are?" he demanded.

"I'm the man who's going to put a bullet into you next time you come sneaking around my place," Dunn said flatly. "And if I was sure you were the one that spooked my horses last night, I'd take it out of your hide."

"Who says it was me?" Sabine demanded.

"Nobody, but I got a good hunch it was you. This time I'll let it pass. I see you on my property again, however, it'll be a different story."

"Reckon I'll come and go as I please," Sabine said in a defiant tone.

"Not across Box B land," Dunn snapped. "That goes for all of you."

"What goes for all of us?"

At the sound of Jack Marr's voice, Dunn turned slowly to one side. He met the tall man's gaze coldly. "The no trespassing signs on my land. You can't see them, but they're there. And they mean every man who works for Diamond X."

Marr shrugged. "You've said that before. Who's disputing it?"

"Ask your gun ranny here," Dunn said. "Let him tell you."

He swung his hard, pressing glance over Sabine and the others, as if assessing their intentions. Apparently satisfied with what he saw, he slid his pistol back into its holster. With no further words, he pivoted on his heel and walked back to his horse. He mounted up, and, with the horse Laura had ridden on a short lead rope, he headed out for his ranch.

He rode at a leisurely pace, coming into his yard around the middle of the afternoon. Abner Loveless awaited him. The white-haired old cowpuncher waddled out from the barn on bowlegs to greet him. He still limped some and the side of his face was now thoroughly discolored.

"Get your business 'tended to?"

"All done," Ben replied.

"You convince Pope that spring was yours?"

Dunn headed into the barn with the two horses. "No sweat at all. Showed him that Land Office map and that's all there was to it. He gave Marr orders to stay clear."

"Good. Glad to hear it's settled. Brung you over a mess of the missus' stew. Set it there on your stove."

"Obliged. Sure appreciate it and you tell your wife so. All this woman cooking is going to spoil me for my own, if I don't look out."

Loveless helped him remove the gear from the horses. That done, he said: "How so?"

"Had a woman . . . a girl here last night that fixed me a fine supper. And breakfast, too."

"A girl?" the old cowpuncher echoed, his brows going up. "Wondered about that extry horse. Who was she and what was she doin' here?"

"Brought her in from Crawford's, where she was stranded. She was going to Pope's."

"What for?"

"Says she's his daughter, Laura."

Loveless was speechless for several moments. He recovered, scrubbed at his head. "Didn't recollect old Isaac ever had a family. 'Course there was the time when I didn't know him. You right sure she's kin?"

Dunn nodded. "Said she was. That's all I know about it."

Finished in the barn, they moved toward the doorway.

Dunn said: "Appreciate your looking after things while I was away. I'll settle with you at the end of the month."

"Forget it," Abner replied. "Were no work to it." He followed Dunn into the yard, shaking his head. "Old Isaac's daughter, eh? Sure does beat all. Reckon Jack ain't goin' to like it much."

"For sure," Ben agreed. "You busy tomorrow? Thought I'd get that wire up around the spring, if you'll help."

"Be glad to," Loveless said. "Late in the mornin' suit you?"

"Fine. And don't forget to thank Hopeful for that stew. *Adiós.*"

"I'll remember," Abner said, and climbed stiffly onto his horse. "So long."

Dunn spent the rest of the day bringing in the remainder of the supplies scattered around his wrecked wagon and doing small chores about the place that needed attention. When darkness came, he entered the house. He put a fire under the stew and the coffee pot, noting the neat and orderly fashion in which Laura had left his kitchen.

He wondered how she had made out with Pope, if she had been able to convince the old rancher that she was his daughter. He hoped so. He would like to think that, at least, Laura would have a good home. He went to bed early and fell asleep quickly.

Shortly after sunup he was in the barn saddling up his buckskin, when a sudden rush of hoofs outside brought him up sharply. Unconsciously his hand dropped to the gun at his hip, as he assured himself that it was ready. He walked into the open. Four riders were drawn up in the yard. He looped the reins of his horse over the rail, continued slowly toward the Diamond X men.

They watched him approach, waited until he was standing only a few feet away.

Marr spoke. "Pretty slick deal you tried to pull, Dunn. Only it's not going to work."

Ben shrugged. "You don't want to take that Land Office map I brought back as proof, then you'd better ride to Santa Fé and look it up yourself," he said, believing their visit had something to do with the spring.

"Not talking about that," Marr stated. "I'm talking about that woman you tried to ring in on us as Pope's daughter."

"Well, isn't she?"

"You know damn' well she's not! I saw through that deal quick. You knew Pope was dying and you come up with this idea to get your hands on his ranch. You and that girl are working together. You figured you could palm her off as his daughter. Then, when he dies, the two of you could take over."

Ben Dunn's shape stiffened as anger swept through him. "That's a lie, and you know it. I never saw the girl until she climbed out of the stage at Crawford's. I brought her along with me and took her to Pope's because she didn't have any other way to get there."

"A good story. You going to tell me now that she didn't spend the night with you here before you brought her over?"

"Sure she stayed here. My team got spooked and ran away. The wagon was turned over. She was hurt a little. Besides, it was too late to go on."

Ben Dunn was growing more furious with each passing moment. Marr's accusations lashed him like a metal-tipped whip.

"Where you got her hid?" Marr demanded. "In that shack or there in the barn?"

"She's not around here," Ben said. "Haven't seen her since I left Pope's. And I don't expect to. Now, get off my place and stay off!"

"Not so fast, friend," Marr said coolly. "You overplayed your hand this time, Dunn. When I'm through with you, you'll wish you'd never seen that girl before. Take a look in the barn, Pete. You try the shack, Bibo. She's around somewhere."

Ben Dunn's pistol came up, centered on Marr. "Be the wrong thing for them to try," he warned.

From off to the left another voice drawled: "Be the wrong thing for you, too, mister. Just drop that iron."

It was a fifth man, one he had not noticed. He was stationed out of sight, beyond the house. Ben let his weapon fall to the ground. He looked up at Marr.

"You're a fool. The girl's not here."

"Maybe. We'll see. And if she's not, we'll take you on to

the marshal, anyway. We'll find her later. She won't get far."

"Marshal?" Dunn said, surprised. "What for?"

"Murder," Jack Marr replied. "For sticking a knife into Isaac Pope last night and killing him."

V

Ben Dunn stared at the tall Marr. Words failed him completely for the moment, and in the hush that followed the accusation the only sounds to be heard were the dry creaks and squeals of leather as Bibo Sabine and Pete Frisco swung from their saddles to do Marr's bidding. Then the fifth man with the rifle drifted deeper into the yard, halting a few steps from Dunn. He reached down, picked up Ben's pistol, thrust it into his own belt.

At last Dunn spoke. "You're a bigger fool than I thought, Marr, or else you're framing this. You know I had nothing to do with Pope's death."

"Only thing I know," the tall man said, "is that it all adds up. You and your lady friend schemed a way to get the Diamond X by claiming she was his kin. Then you got Pope out of the way so you could take over."

The wild fury within Ben Dunn had blown itself out. Now there was only a hard core of seething anger. He glanced about through shuttered eyes. Marr had not drawn his pistol, nor had the fourth man. The only gun on him was the rifle held by the rider who stood a few paces away. He calculated his chances for escape. The greatest risk lay in the fact that no horse, upon which he might flee, was handy, and it would be senseless to attempt a break on foot, even if he could somehow move fast enough to get his hands on the rifle.

Bibo Sabine came from the house at that moment. He halted just outside the door. "She ain't in there, Jack."

Marr said: "Look around the yard. Maybe she's in one of

the sheds or hiding in the brush."

Sabine turned to do as he was told, walking in that awkward way of saddle men, unaccustomed to being on foot and disliking every moment of it. Pete Frisco emerged from the barn.

"Ain't nobody in here!" he yelled. "Looked good."

Marr nodded. "All right. Bring Dunn's horse up here. Then help Bibo."

The thick-shouldered Frisco led Ben's buckskin to where they had gathered. He handed the reins to Dunn, wheeled about, and struck out across the yard after Sabine.

"Mount up," Marr ordered. "Don't get any ideas, unless you want to die quick. I'd as soon haul you in dead as alive."

"Expect you'd like dead better," Dunn said dryly, and stepped into his saddle.

Again he looked about. He was considerably better off now. On a horse his chances for escape were much improved, but there was still the problem of having no gun. He was not looking beyond the immediate need to get away, to get free of Marr and his riders. After that was accomplished, he could sit back and think the matter through, decide what must be done.

The minutes dragged slowly by. Sabine and Frisco were somewhere behind the barn, poking about in the brush and weeds. The fourth man stirred uncomfortably as the gradually rising heat and inactivity began to wear on him. "Sure don't look like she's around here."

Marr said: "Maybe not, Charlie, but we're going to be sure. Got to find her."

"You figure she come this way? You find tracks or something?"

Marr shook his head. "Didn't look for any. Where else

would she go? Only other place she knew around here was Dunn's. She wouldn't just take off across the flats."

"Reckon you're right," Charlie mumbled.

Sabine and Frisco appeared at the far corner of the barn. Marr pivoted his attention to the man with the rifle. "Get your horse, Harvey."

The cowboy wheeled off at once, started for his mount that stood, apparently, somewhere in the brush beyond the house. Ben Dunn realized his moment was suddenly at hand. He threw a glance at Sabine and Frisco, another at the departing Harvey. He was the dangerous one. Ben set himself in the saddle.

It was a good twenty-five yards to the nearest stand of shrubbery—and possible escape—but he would chance it. He would act the instant Harvey was out of sight and while Frisco and Sabine were still at the far side of the yard. At that moment he would have only Jack Marr and the cowboy called Charlie to contend with.

Tension built with the fleeting seconds. It would be a tight squeeze. With each step away Harvey took, Frisco and Sabine drew a pace closer. He sought to estimate the position of the two gunmen when Harvey turned the corner of the house. Somewhere near the yard's dead center, he figured. He would be within range of their handguns. He must endeavor to put Marr and Charlie in between them and himself when he made his move.

From the tail of his eye he saw the rider with the rifle reach the corner, turn. Methodically he counted, allowing time for Harvey to get a distance beyond. He drove spurs into the buckskin. The startled horse plunged forward, straight at Marr.

Dunn yelled, adding to the confusion. The buckskin veered to avoid colliding with Marr's gray that shied off frantically. He came up against Charlie's mount and reared suddenly.

"Get him!" Marr yelled, savagely fighting his horse.

Bibo Sabine's shout came from the yard close by. Dunn, crouched low on the leaping buckskin, did not look around. These were the critical moments—the time it would take him to gain the shelter of the brush. He expected to hear the crash of gunshots. There were none. Evidently he had succeeded in maneuvering Marr and Charlie into a position where they blocked the two gunmen. Harvey, the rider with the rifle, was the big question—would he hear, turn, and reach the center of the yard in time to lay down a shot?

The buckskin was covering ground in huge strides. It was a short distance to the brush, but to Dunn it seemed like miles. Back of him he could hear Marr cursing in a steady flow, interspersing the scathing words with commands. A gun suddenly cracked through the morning. Charlie, he suspected. The bullet droned by, *thunked* dully into a small tree just beyond Dunn. He crowded down tighter on the buckskin's heaving body—only ten feet more.

He reached the first stand of brush as several guns opened up. Wild bullets, clipping viciously through the leaves and other foliage behind him, told him they could not see his exact position. He kept low, raced on, driving the buckskin recklessly down a shallow ravine that drained away to the right.

Marr and the others were getting under way. The shooting ceased, and he was aware of the pounding of their horses in pursuit. But he breathed easier. In a chase, on his own land where he was familiar with every foot of ground, his chances were better than good. But he must try to keep from their sight. No man could outrun a bullet.

He swept down the arroyo, swung hard left where it flattened out into another. He did not look back. There was no need. The hammering of the running horses kept him well informed. He looked ahead. He was heading back toward Comanche Mountain now. There was no safety out in the open, on the flat country. The rugged, rocky, and thickly overgrown cañons and ridges of the mountain itself were his safest bet.

He pressed the buckskin for more speed. The game little horse responded and drove on, but he could not be expected to maintain such a pace for long. The grade was growing steeper, the footing more uncertain. The possibilities of the horse's stumbling increased with every stride.

Dunn risked a look over his shoulder. He must know how near Marr and the others were. He saw them as he turned. They were just rounding a curve in the arroyo he was following. It was their first glimpse of him. Three guns broke out as one.

Ben again heard the whine of death as the bullets whirred past, this time much too close. He saw spurts of dust ahead as they struck the ground, heard their scream as they ricocheted off into space. He jerked the buckskin sharply to one side, throwing a screen of brush across their rear. The horse was beginning to heave, to tremble from his running. He could not go much farther.

A narrow corridor between high-piled rocks appeared to his left. Without hesitation, he veered into it. It slanted gently back downgrade, gave the buckskin some relief from his climbing. The passageway ran a dozen yards, ending abruptly against a thick stand of scrub oak. Dead end! The horse slid to a halt.

The hair on Ben Dunn's neck began to prickle and stiffen. He would be trapped if Marr and his riders were to spot the turn-off and elect to follow it. He slipped from the heaving buckskin, crept forward a few steps, and listened. Off to the right, he could hear them thundering up the trail. Marr's voice shouted something. It was almost drowned by the horses, and Dunn could not distinguish the words.

The sound swept on. He realized a moment later that they had missed the turn and were continuing on up the slope of Comanche Mountain. He trotted back to his horse, mounted up. He returned to the main trail, headed downward. They would soon discover their error, he knew, but he would not be where they could find him. He knew exactly where he would go—on the topmost ridge of the mountain.

VI

He allowed the buckskin to pick its way slowly along the foot of the mountain, keeping well hidden within the maze of brush and rock. Higher up on the slope, he could hear faintly the shouts of Jack Marr and his men as they combed through the rough area. They had split, it seemed to him, and were now searching individually. He was safe, at least for the time. He was far below them, making a long swing toward the opposite end of the mountain.

He wished there had been time to get himself a gun, but the only available one was back at the ranch and that would have meant exposing himself. The Diamond X men would certainly spot him and come boiling down the slope to box him in before he could get away a second time. He would have to do without a weapon. All he could do was to stay hidden, permit Marr and his riders to hunt themselves out. When they would be gone, he could move about freely.

He reached the spring over which he and Isaac Pope had quarreled, halted there long enough to water the buckskin and have a drink himself. When that was done, he headed up a long cañon that slashed diagonally across the body of Comanche Mountain. High, steep walls here closed in on him from two sides, but he had no fears. Marr was a considerable distance to the east of him and could, in no way, look down into the gash where he moved.

It was familiar ground to Ben Dunn. He had climbed the narrow cañon wall before, knew it would lead him eventually to the base of the rimrock that capped the mountain. From it he could reach the only break in the ridge whereby a man could gain the summit. It was an old game trail, likely unknown to anyone but himself and the long-eared mule deer that used it. At its upper end, the walls of the cañon began to lower. The trail became a series of rock ledges. Dunn dismounted. From that point he proceeded on foot. It was unsafe to ride the buckskin any farther. The horse would have a difficult enough time maintaining his footing on the smooth, rain-washed rock without the extra burden of a rider.

It was well into the afternoon when he reached the top, breaking out into the broad, grassy meadow that lay behind the ridge. It was a beautiful plateau, thrust high into the heavens, clear and blue as a flawless diamond. Grass was knee-deep everywhere, shifting gently back and forth with the whim of the breeze like a vast sheet of undulating silver. It extended for miles in all directions, carpeting the crater-like top of Comanche Mountain.

Ben allowed the buckskin to wander out into the grass. He cut back, climbed a slight peak, and turned his attention eastward, onto the direction where Marr and his men would be. Flowing out beneath him and the many-colored facets of the rimrock was the first, steep slope of the mountain. It ended several hundred yards down, where it bulged slightly and resumed a more gentle descent. The entire face of Comanche Mountain was studded with pines, firs, and other growth as well as with rocks of varying sizes. This prevented him from locating Marr and the others.

By studying the land and its formations, and from his personal knowledge of the country, he eventually sighted the general area where he could expect them to be. He marked that particular section in his mind by sighting a dead juniper tree that clung precariously to the edge of the rim. He dropped back to the buckskin, mounted, rode east-

ward through the turbulent sea of grass until he was opposite the marker. There he again turned loose the horse that
would not drift far in such excellent grazing. Dunn then
made his way to the ridge.

Before he was fully on the rim, he heard a man's hoarse
shout. He removed his hat, dropped flat to the ground, and
crawled to the juniper. He looked down. At first he saw
nothing. Moments later he watched two riders emerge from
the trees, halting in a small clearing far below. The man on
the gray horse unquestionably was Jack Marr. The other he
could not recognize at such a distance. As he watched, a
third man entered the open ground. He was followed moments later by two more. There were now five in all, the entire group that had been in his yard earlier.

They remained gathered for some time, having a discussion of some sort. When they broke apart a few minutes
later, Marr, with one rider, turned back down the mountain. The remaining three split and disappeared once again
into the rock and brush.

It was evident to Ben what was taking place. Marr and
one man, probably Bibo Sabine, were abandoning the
search. The other three men would continue. They now
were moving west across the slope of the mountain, a
course that would eventually bring them to a dead end on
the rim of the deep cañon. There was nothing to fear from
them, unless he permitted himself to be seen and thus revealed his position. They could do nothing when they came
to the cañon except turn back and retrace their trail.

Dunn laid back, his eyes turned upward to the cloudless
arch overhead. In the arid, towering world atop Comanche
Mountain sound carried with startling clarity. He could
easily hear the buckskin cropping contentedly at the grass,
the far-off moaning of a dove, the rapid clacking of an in-

sect a few hundred yards up the ridge. Turning that way, he saw motion, saw it freeze. He beheld a buck mule deer, with a wide spread of antlers, herding his harem of does. All were etched against a background of grays and greens.

He remained absolutely still, enjoying the sight. When the old buck did not again see anything of a suspicious nature, he sauntered on, trailed obediently by his mincing retinue. They soon were lost in the tall grass.

Dunn whiled away the remainder of the afternoon, and, when it was nearly dark, he came off the ridge and headed back for his ranch. He knew there was little if any chance of running into Marr's men at this late hour. They would have long ago given up the search.

He must find Laura and help her. That she had somehow managed to escape Marr was clear. Where could she have gone to hide? She was a stranger in the country and would know little of it. She must be somewhere between his own Box B holdings and Diamond X. It was the only area she had been through. Marr had seemed to believe she had come to his place. Wherever she was, she must be found. He was the only friend she had—the only one who could help her.

First he must have a gun. It would be foolish to begin a search without a weapon. One of Marr's riders, the one they called Harvey, had picked up his revolver when Ben had been compelled to drop it. There was no point in looking for it in the yard. But that was of no great consequence. The mate to it was in the footlocker in his house. There had been a time when he had carried two guns.

He worked his way carefully through the brush and rock, and, when he drew near the buildings of the Box B, he halted within the thick brush that rimmed the yard. There was every chance that Marr had left men to keep an eye on the place. Still, he could see no horses or hear any suspicious sounds.

It was too quiet, and to believe that Marr had not set men to watch the ranch was foolhardy. He tied the buckskin well back in the brush, hoping he would not sense the nearness of his stable mates in the barn and give his presence away. Dunn began to work in closer.

He remembered the old rifle and a handful of shells he kept in the barn. He had placed them there at one time for use on coyotes and wolves which occasionally slunk in from the mountain in search of a calf or other easy meal. He decided it was a better gamble to try for it than enter the house for the six-gun. Accordingly he dropped back, circled wide, and came up to the barn on its blind side. It was a simple matter to crawl through the window and gain entrance.

Once inside, he paused to listen. He heard only the muted breathing of the horses, an occasional dry rasp as they changed positions and rubbed against the sides of their stalls. Dunn moved softly into the runway. He stayed close to the wall, where the shadows were deepest, made his way to the front of the barn. The rifle should be hanging on a peg just inside the door. The cartridges would be lying nearby on the wooden crosspiece that braced the studding.

He came to the end of the runway. He saw the rifle. It was on the opposite side. Moonlight striking through the open doorway laid danger across his path. To get the rifle meant exposing himself to anyone who might be watching at that moment, either from the inside of the barn, or outside. But he needed the rifle. He stepped boldly into the flood of light, moving quickly.

"Ben!"

The summons reached out of the darkness, caught him in stride. It was the voice of Laura Pope.

VII

He hesitated only momentarily, then completed the distance to the rifle and ammunition. Casting a long look at the dark bulk of his house, he wheeled, swiftly re-crossed the runway, and retreated into the darkness at the rear of the barn.

"Ben," Laura said again. "I'm over here."

He pivoted at the sound of her voice. It came from behind stacked sacks of grain in an unused stall. She rose to meet him.

"Didn't ever expect to find you here," he said. "Was about to start out and hunt."

"I came as soon as it was dark. I don't think anyone saw me."

"Anybody been around?"

"Three men. The one they call Pete and two others."

"That would be Frisco, with Harvey and Charlie. They would have stopped by for a look when they came off the mountain. How about Marr?"

"Haven't seen him since I left the ranch."

He walked back to the runway, to a position where he could see the yard and keep an eye on the house. Laura followed.

"You know Isaac Pope is dead?"

"Yes, I know," she replied in a toneless voice.

He turned, took her shoulders between his two hands. She was near the breaking point. "Everything's going to be all right now," he said. "You know they're accusing us of doing it?"

She looked up at him. "I didn't know about you. I'm sorry about it."

"We're both in on it. Marr and his bunch were here. Claims you and I framed the whole thing . . . that we're working together. He says we cooked up this daughter thing so you could inherit the Pope Ranch. Then we killed Pope."

She brushed at her eyes. "It's unbelievable! It's all happened so fast. . . ."

"You have any idea who might have killed Pope?"

"No, I haven't," she said. "When I saw him last, he was alive."

"This thing's going to be hard to clear up," Dunn said in a thoughtful voice. "Be tough to scrape up proof that will point to the real killer."

"I'm sorry I dragged you into it," Laura said. "Seems I've caused you nothing but trouble from the very first."

"Forget it," he replied. "You said I was a friend. I intend to prove it's true . . . maybe that I'm even more than just that."

She gave him no answer, only moved closer to him. After a time she asked: "What do we do next?"

"I've got to put you where you'll be safe," he said. "Think the best idea is to get you to Salt River. That's the nearest town where there's people and a hotel. And the marshal's got his office there. Marr's plan was to take us to him and make his charge of murder against us. If we can get there first and tell him our side of the story, maybe we'll have a good chance of clearing things up."

She stepped back from him. "But I have no proof to show him, no way to back up my story that Isaac Pope was my father. Wouldn't we be playing right into Marr's hands?"

Dunn frowned in the darkness. "That letter and the picture you told me about, they're still at the Pope place?"

"Yes," she said. "There was no time to get anything."

He considered that for a time. Then: "How did you get here? You didn't walk all the way?"

"No, I had a horse. At least, I started with one. I was up and dressed early. I heard Marr and someone talking. It was right after they found my father dead. I listened and learned that they thought I had something to do with it and that they were coming to get me. I slipped out of a window. There were some horses tied up at the rail. I took one and got away before they realized it."

"They follow you?"

"Yes, but I had several minutes' start. They began to catch up, and I pulled off into the brush and hid. My horse broke away after they passed, and I had to go on, on foot. It wasn't far from here. Only two or three miles."

"That must have been about the time they rode in here," Dunn said. "Marr figured, when he missed you, that you probably came straight to me. I'm glad that you did."

He moved off toward the stalls where the horses rested. "I'll saddle a mount for you. My buckskin is waiting out there in the brush. We'll head for Salt River early as we can."

She was silent while he threw the gear on one of the bays. That finished, he again looked toward the house. "Have to get us some grub. Full day's ride to the town. I haven't had anything since this morning, and I expect you haven't, either. Then we'll need some for the trail. Nothing to do but chance it."

"Chance what?"

"That none of Marr's bunch is hanging around, watching the place." He picked up the rifle, cracked its mechanism to check the chamber. There was a cartridge in place. "Stay here, keep in the dark," he said, and dropped back to the window through which he had previously made an entrance.

He leaped softly to the ground, paused a moment to listen. He heard nothing, and crossed the length of the building. At its corner he went to his hands and knees, crawled swiftly along the fringe of brush to a point directly behind the ranch house. Again he waited a time. He heard no unusual sounds, and, still crouched, he dashed across the open ground, gaining the rear of the structure.

There was no possibility of entering through a back window, as he had done at the barn. All were too small. There was a side door to one of the rooms he had built on, but it was securely barred. It would be useless to attempt to force it. His one means was through the front.

He circled the house, keeping in the shadows of the brush, halting when he was in a position to see the door. It was clearly visible in the moon-flooded night, as was the open yard across which he would have to make his way. If anyone were watching the house, it would be impossible for a man to reach that door unnoticed.

The faint jingle of metal stiffened him. He raised up, listened intently. He heard then the dry creak of leather.

He sank down slowly, went to his belly. Flat on the ground, he considered what must be done. The sound had originated off to his right, not far away. Jack Marr had left a guard, just as Ben had suspected he might. Likely there was only one. With him out of the way, he could complete the necessary preparations for the trip to Salt River. Then Laura and he could be on the trail.

He worked his way silently off through the dark, making only a short distance at a time. It was a tedious process but finally he saw the horse, tethered to a small tree. The man was a short distance beyond it. He had settled down, his back against a stump. His head was dropped forward on his arms that were crossed upon his knees. He was sleeping soundly.

Dunn raised himself carefully, probed the night for a second horse and another sentry. He could see no evidence of either. At that moment the horse got wind of him. He jerked his head up sharply. The clear jingle of bridle metal broke the silence. The sleeping man awoke with a start. He glanced about, seeing Ben. He clawed at the pistol on his hip. Dunn moved in like a swiftly descending shadow. He brought the rifle down in a short arc. It thudded against the man's head, and he collapsed without a sound.

Dunn knelt over him, rolled him onto his back. It was the one they had called Harvey. Ben's fingers explored along his belt, found what he knew should be there—his own revolver. He slid it into his empty holster, looked more closely at the cowboy. He would be out for some time.

He wheeled, trotted back the route he had come, still cautious to stay in the dark areas. There was the possibility that Marr had left two, or even three men, to watch. He would take no greater risks than necessary. He reached the corner of the house, halted there for a time while he searched the brush beyond the moonlit yard. He could see nothing, and, delaying no longer, he crossed to the door and hurriedly let himself inside.

Immediately he began to gather the needed items: his saddlebags, a canteen of water, coffee pot, a sack of coffee beans, bread, dried meat, two tins of peaches, a handful of potatoes. Stowing all but the container of water in the leather pouches, he went back to the door. All was quiet outside. He left quickly, still trusting only to the shadows, and returned to the barn.

Inside, he found Laura waiting where he had left her. He threw the saddlebags across the horse he had selected for her, jammed the rifle into the boot.

"Marr left a man to watch the house. Could be there's another. We better get out of here fast."

"What happened? Did you have to . . . ?"

"Only a rap on the head. He'll be quiet for a spell, long enough for us to get going."

He backed the bay out into the runway. "We'll have to use the door," he said. "There's no opening in the back of this barn big enough for a horse. If Harvey was the only man Marr left, we'll have no trouble. If there's another, we may have to run for it."

She said: "I understand."

"Mount up," he said, dropping back to assist her. "Then you'll be ready to ride if need be. My horse is behind the barn. I'll lead the way."

Laura settled herself in the saddle with no comment. Dunn took the reins in his left hand, leaving the right free, and started for the doorway. They reached the opening. He halted briefly, and then stepped out into the yard. There he again paused, half expecting to hear the crash of a gun, feel the smash of a bullet. There were only the distant murmurs of night birds in the trees.

He moved out again, walked fast. They gained the corner of the barn without incident, turned, passed along its length. A minute later they were within the safety of the brush. Either Marr had picketed only Harvey to watch, or else the other also was asleep. They reached the buckskin and halted. Dunn took the saddlebags laid across the girl's horse and fastened them securely to his own gear. He anchored the canteen to the horn. Finished, he glanced up at Laura. A shaft of silver moonlight cutting through the leaves of an overspreading tree fell across her face, pointing up its soft beauty. She was looking off into the night.

"Been a bad day for you," he said, stepping onto his horse. "We'll travel for an hour or so, and then stop. I know a spot where we can rest for a time and have a bite to eat."

VIII

In the stillness that followed his words, there was only the far-away, lonely sound of a bird calling into the dark of the night. He glanced at her, wondered if exhaustion had at last caught up with her, if she were asleep. She saw him turn and smiled wanly.

He reached out, took the reins of her horse into his hand. He touched the buckskin with spurs, and they moved out immediately, the bay holding back a little but following, nevertheless.

They rode steadily for a lengthy hour, and then pulled into a small clearing that fronted a cave-like opening in the base of the mountain. Holding to her horse, Dunn swung down.

"We'll rest here until it's lighter. I'll make coffee."

Wearily she twisted about. He helped her to the ground, and she walked to the edge of the hollow, gouged from the slope as though by some gigantic hand, and sat down. He secured the horses in the brush beyond the cleared area and returned, bringing with him the saddlebags and canteen. He built a small fire, placed the sooty pot, half filled with water, over the flames. He began to rummage through the food he had provided.

"Be just a few minutes," he said to her. "And it won't be much, but it will do until we get to Salt River. Good café there. We'll have a real supper then."

She smiled at him, expressing her thanks. He turned to his chore. From the saddlebags he obtained some dried meat, several hard biscuits. He opened a tin of peaches, poured half into a cup for her. The coffee boiled up. He removed it from the fire, tipped back the lid. With a twig, he stirred down the froth. After it had settled, he poured two cups. He moved to her side, placing the food before her.

"Thank you," she murmured. "That coffee smells so good."

"One thing I can guarantee"—he grinned—"is that it's strong enough!"

Both were hungry and they ate steadily. The food was simple, but ample and filling. When they had finished, he replaced the cups and what was left of the food in the saddlebags, and then returned to her. He settled down, rolled himself a cigarette.

"You didn't ask me what happened when I saw my father," she said. "Aren't you interested in knowing whether he accepted me as his daughter or not?"

He shook his head. "Reckon it doesn't matter. If you are Laura Pope or someone else, it made no difference. I just figured you were and let it go at that."

"And if I had been an imposter, someone just trying to inherit the Pope Ranch like that man Crawford thought?"

"Like I said, it would make no difference. I'm interested in you . . . not who you are."

She moved nearer to him, placing her hand on his arm. She leaned forward, kissing him lightly on the cheek. "I'm afraid to think of how it might have been, if I hadn't met you," she said.

"Haven't done much good for you, yet," he said. "And we're not finished with this thing."

"I'm not afraid," she said. "Long as we're together, I know it will all work out."

He did not reply. She watched him draw deeply on his cigarette, then exhale slowly. She said: "Mister Pope accepted me as his daughter before he was murdered. It was all settled. After he read my mother's letter and saw the picture likeness, he talked for a while. He had some papers in a box near his bed. They seemed to prove something to him. Anyway, he was convinced. And just before I left his room, he mentioned a trunk in which he said there were some more pictures, tintypes. We were going to get them out today."

"That's fine," Dunn said. "I'm glad you were able to prove it to him . . . and that he got to see you before he was killed. After all, you are his only child. Did he talk with Marr after that?"

"I don't know. I expect he did."

"Marr would have had to hear it from somebody. Likely it was Pope who told him. And that started things turning in Marr's head. He saw the Diamond X slipping out of his hands, and he had to figure a way to hold it."

"Then he . . . ?"

Ben Dunn came up swiftly. He lifted his hand, closing off the girl's words. Back, somewhere along the route they had traveled, he had heard a noise—the distinct *click* of metal striking against rock.

Laura looked at him questioningly. He shook his head, warning her to silence. It was hard to believe Marr, or any of his men, could have got onto their trail so quickly and could have located them in the night. He thought of the fire he had built. There was the answer. Even a small one created a glow. They must have noticed it.

He drew his pistol, carefully scraped earth and trash over the now smoldering embers with the toe of his boot. He continued to listen, head cocked in the direction of the sound. There was nothing. It could have been a deer, he reasoned, or it might have been a horse and rider.

He glided silently to Laura. "Wait here," he whispered, "but if I'm not back in a couple of minutes, or if you hear sounds of trouble, get out of here fast. Ride straight west. I'll find you."

She nodded her understanding. He moved off at once into the silver-shot night. He kept to the dark shadows. It was slow going. He must avoid contact with brush that would scrape against him, set up a noise. He covered a hundred yards, and froze. The sound of a horse, blowing impatiently, reached him.

He remained rigid for a long minute, considering his best course of action. It was reasonable to think that the sound had been made by a stray horse, one wandering about on the foot of Comanche Mountain. But he could assume nothing, take nothing for granted. He must know. He moved forward again with even greater care. He knew the approximate location of the animal now. That made it easier.

"That fire sure was around in here somewheres!"

Dunn hauled up short, blocked by the sudden, distinct declaration, as effectively as if he had walked into a rock wall. It was Bibo Sabine's voice. The man could be no farther away than a wagon's length.

"Seems to me it was higher up."

Pete Frisco. Dunn wondered if there were more. He could see none of them. They were beyond a dense stand of cedar and scrub oak and on a lower level of the slope.

"What you say, Harvey? You figure they're higher up, or lower down?"

"My guess'd be they're up high. That's how come we seen the glow. And Dunn would want to be where he could see good."

"Play hell seein' much at night from anywhere," Sabine said.

66

"He'll be holed up, waitin' for daylight. Then him and the girl will move out. He'd pick a spot where he could watch from, sure enough."

"Reckon it don't matter," Frisco said. "Jack wants 'em both. We got to find 'em."

Dunn eased silently back in the darkness. He and Laura were on an almost direct line with the three riders. If they delayed longer, they would be discovered.

"Let's just keep ridin' the way we was," Sabine suggested. "But spread out like. And keep watchin' up the side of the mountain. Maybe we can spot that fire again."

Dunn pulled farther into the brush. He broke into a trot. He knew he was running the risk of tripping, of dislodging loose shale and creating a disturbance. But it could not be helped. He must get Laura out of the area fast. The three men would blunder down upon them in a very few minutes.

"You hear somethin'?" Sabine's question came to him clearly. "Sounded like it was just ahead, somewheres in them bushes."

Dunn broke into the clearing. The noise of Sabine and the other men approaching now was plain in the hush. He halted, glancing about. Laura was not there. His saddlebags, the canteen, and the coffee pot lay where he had left them. He snatched up the water container and the bags, ignoring all else. Laura, likely, was with the horses. He plunged across the open ground for the thicket where he had left their mounts. Only the buckskin remained. Laura, heeding his warning, had fled.

It was just as well. But he must be certain. He moved to the buckskin, throwing the saddlebags and canteen into place.

"Laura," he whispered into the darkness.

There was no reply. He stepped to the saddle, probed

the dark shrubbery with anxious eyes. "Laura!" he repeated, raising his voice.

The night yielded no answer. He could delay no longer, and there was no question the girl had gone. He moved out.

"Over there!"

Bibo Sabine's hoarse voice was like a sharp sword thrust through the darkness. "There he is . . . edge of that clearin'!"

A gun blast shattered the stillness. Ben heard the *shriek* of a bullet, the sudden pound of onrushing horses only yards away.

"Circle around!" Sabine yelled. "Cut him off 'fore he can get away!"

Dunn spun the buckskin about in a tight circle. He drove home his spurs. The horse plunged ahead, crashed through a low hedge of scrub oak, stumbled, caught himself, and went on. Another gun smashed through the whirling confusion. Ben flung a glance to the clearing. Through the lacework of moonlight and shadows he saw the three riders converge. It was too dark to tell which was which, but it did not matter.

He jerked the buckskin hard right, headed down the grade. Instantly one of the cowboys fired. The bullet *caromed* off the trunk of a nearby pine tree, wailed into space. He swerved the buckskin to the left, driving hard, recklessly. The horse was racing madly through the night, plunging through brush, stumbling, leaping over fallen logs. His ears were laid flat, long neck extended.

"Keep after 'em! Keep 'em runnin'!"

Sabine's horse commands were like a cracking whip to the rear. He apparently thought Laura was with him, Dunn realized. Dunn was thankful she was not. She could never have stayed on the saddle through such a nightmarish ride.

He was striking upgrade now, climbing the slope of Comanche Mountain. He could not continue for long. It was much too difficult for the buckskin. He was slowing down, and, in so doing, Dunn realized he was presenting Sabine and the two riders with an easy target.

He sliced back immediately, not to the right again—that would have taken him in the direction he had been following—but to the left, thus doubling back. He reasoned that such a move would be unexpected by Marr's riders and it would also pull them off Laura who was somewhere farther to the west.

Sabine was too close to be misled. He saw Ben change directions, snapped a quick shot. The bullet struck somewhere behind the saddle horn, ricocheted noisily into the forest. The sound gouged the buckskin's shattered nerves. He shied, came to a plunging, skidding halt, almost catapulting Dunn from his back.

Dunn jabbed at the confused animal's ribs mercilessly. The horse righted himself, cut straight down the slope, heading directly for Sabine and the others. It was useless and too late to try and stop him. Dunn dragged out his own gun. Sabine was abruptly before him. He threw a bullet at the rider, saw that he had missed, and was carried on in a wild rush by his crazed horse.

Instantly the three men opened up at him. The night was suddenly filled with screaming lead, echoing blasts. Dunn, twisting and dodging to avoid being swept from the saddle by low-hanging branches and dragged to the ground by clawing brush, struggled to stay with the buckskin. Each second he expected to feel the searing shock of a bullet driving into his body.

The horse swerved to avoid a solid wall of brush. In the next instant he felt the buckskin quiver, stagger to one side.

He had been hit. The horse reared, pawed the air frantically with his forelegs. He began to fall back, go down into the bushes.

Dunn leaped clear. He struck on all fours. He was up instantly, plunging off into the darkness. Behind him rose the shouts of Sabine, Frisco, and Harvey. They had seen the buckskin go down, thought he was under the threshing animal. He did not look back to see if they had stopped. He rushed on down the steep grade, his long legs taking monstrous strides as momentum lent him speed. He was inviting disaster at every step. He fought to slow down and maintain balance, but he was like a leaf caught in a blast of wind.

The crash of the riders through the brush was loud again. They had discovered he was not with the luckless buckskin and was again seeking escape. He slanted off to his left. If he could reach the big cañon, he might have a chance. In that wild and badly overgrown area there were many places where a man could hide.

He plunged on recklessly, speed unchecked. He tried to keep in the shadows, but there was little choice in direction on his part. He fought to stay out of the open where Sabine and the others could get a shot at his back.

"There he goes!"

It was Pete Frisco who yelled. Ben hauled himself to one side, sought to destroy any target he might be presenting. All three riders fired together, orange flashes marking their positions. They were close—too close to him.

Abruptly, right under his feet it seemed, the ragged edge of an arroyo yawned. It was impossible to check his head-long speed. He leaped, trusted to luck that the ravine was not too wide and that he would find safe footing on its far side. His boots hit the opposite wall. In that identical moment his body crashed into a small tree or bush of some sort, he did not know which. He felt himself hurled backward. He clawed frantically to catch himself, failed, dropped back into the deep slash.

"Look out!" Bibo Sabine's warning came from directly overhead.

He struck the ground just as the three horses leaped over the arroyo, soared above him in a clatter of displaced gravel and rattling brush, then thundered on.

He lay still for several seconds, sucking for breath. He was flat on his back in the sandy floor of the ravine. He had been lucky. He was unhurt, and the three riders, apparently having seen him leap, thought he had successfully cleared the arroyo and was still going, somewhere in the darkness of the opposite side. They had not witnessed his fall.

He could not stay there. He realized that and struggled to his feet. When they did not again locate him, they would come back. He started down the arroyo at a trot, electing to stay within its depth. It was not hard going, but he was still short of breath from the hard run and the fall. The ravine should lead him to the cañon, he figured. Once there his chances of survival would be greatly improved.

He rounded a sharp curve in the arroyo. The dark, indefinite outline of something—of a horse, slowed his steps. It was standing broadside in the narrow slash. A strange sort of dread, an emotion unfamiliar to Dunn, clutched at his throat. It was the bay he had provided for Laura. Where was she? What had happened?

He hurried to the patient animal that swung his long head about, watched him run up with stolid indifference. The girl was not nearby. He looked about thoroughly. He took the bay's reins, continued on for another ten yards. Then he saw her. She lay at the foot of the ravine's steep

71

bank. She had not been as fortunate as he when her horse attempted to clear the arroyo.

He rushed to her, knelt beside her still, crumpled form. He turned her over gently, peered down into the pale oval of her face. A terrible fear gripped him. She looked so calm, so white. He lowered his head, placing his ear to her lips. A feeling of relief slipped through him. She was breathing. He placed his arm under her shoulders, raising her slightly. An ugly bruise was beginning to darken the side of her head, just above the left cheek bone. A ragged, raw scratch could be traced down her neck where an outthrusting branch had clawed her.

He glanced hurriedly around. He needed water for her. But there was no spring nearby, and the canteen was on the saddle of his buckskin. He began to chafe her wrists with brisk, hard motions. She stirred in the cradle of his arm. Her lids fluttered, opened. Her eyes at first filled with alarm, and then calmed as she recognized him.

"Oh, Ben. . . ."

He laid a finger across her lips, silencing her. "Quiet, Marr's bunch is around close. We can't make any noise. Are you hurt?"

She stirred in his arms. "I don't think so. My shoulder feels a little numb."

"You've got a bad bruise on your face, too. How did it happen?"

She explored the side of her head gingerly. "I don't exactly know. One minute I was riding, heading west like you told me to. Next thing I was sailing through the air."

That accounted for the bay's coming through unhurt. He had simply stopped short when he saw the arroyo. Laura had been thrown over his head. It was fortunate she had struck mostly on the soft sand, not higher up against the ragged-edged rocks and stiff brush.

"Think you can ride?" he asked. "We've got to get away from here. Sabine and his bunch will find us if we stay."

She said: "I'll manage. Was that who it was back there?"

"Sabine, Frisco, and the one they call Harvey."

He got to his feet, helped her rise. They stood there for a short time, she testing her strength, Dunn listening to the night. He thought he could hear Sabine and the others, but he was not sure. In any event, he could take no chances.

He wheeled to the bay, led him up to her. He helped her swing into the saddle. She looked about questioningly.

"Where's your horse?"

"Back on the mountain," he said. "Stopped a bullet. I'll lead you out of this cañon, then we'll have to ride double."

"Are we still going to Salt River?"

"Not much chance now," he said, and moved out ahead of the bay. "This horse would never make it, carrying us both. And we've got no water or grub."

She considered his words for a time. "Then what can we do?"

The trail was rough, indistinct. Dunn was forced to go carefully. He said: "Some people by the name of Loveless have a place a few miles farther on. They're friends of mine. We'll head there. I've been thinking about that idea I had of going to the marshal. Could be it wasn't so good. Seems I recall that Marr and him are pretty close friends. Without anything to back up our story, we might have a hard time making him see things our way."

"Can the Lovelesses help us?"

"They'll do all they can, but Abner is an old man. Sabine roughed him up some a few days ago. I don't want to get them too mixed up in this, because it would bring them a lot of trouble."

Laura said: "I see."

They were approaching the end of the arroyo. Here it would be necessary to climb out onto nearly level land. He led the bay, with Laura clinging tightly to the saddle horn as her mount scrambled up the last few feet of the trail, on to a fairly level meadow. He halted there, allowed the horse to recover himself while he turned his attention to their back trail. There were no signs of Marr's men, but he could not be entirely sure. Night masked all movement, even at a short distance. Still, it worked both ways; if he could not see them, they would have no better luck spotting Laura and him.

He swung up onto the bay behind the girl. The horse moved off, walking slowly through the short grass. The animal was tired, and the extra burden of Dunn was unwelcome. He held up, reluctant to proceed. Dunn goaded him gently with his spurs, and, finally, the bay continued.

Laura leaned back, relaxed in the circle of his arms. "I'll be so thankful when this is all over with," she murmured.

"It won't be long," he answered.

IX

The Loveless place was dark, as he had expected it would be. It was still an hour or more until daylight and the elderly couple would yet be asleep. He rode into the small, clean-swept yard, headed the weary bay toward the corral behind the house. Laura had given in to exhaustion, had sagged against him and dozed for the last several miles. When he halted the horse, she awakened with a start.

"Where are we?"

"At Abner's," he said, dropping off the bay. He extended his hands to help her dismount. The night had turned chilly and she was shivering.

"Be just a minute," he said. "Got to put up this horse. He's had a hard time of it. I'll fix some coffee when we get inside."

She nodded her understanding, stepped back and watched while he loosed the bay's saddle and removed it and the bridle. The horse headed wearily into the square of axed logs and began at once to eat a pile of hay thrown into one corner. Dunn returned and with Laura entered the house.

It was little more than a shack, constructed mostly of cast-off lumber, tarpaper, mud bricks, and logs. It consisted of one large room, which served as kitchen, dining area, and living room. Sleeping quarters for the couple was a separate section built off one end. Once inside, Dunn stepped softly across the central room and quietly closed the slab door that divided the two.

"No use waking them up," he said in a low whisper. He

pointed to a rawhide chair. "Sit down and rest. I'll get the stove going."

Laura did as he directed, and he turned to the cast-iron range. With little noise, he got a fire going. Once that was done, he took the granite coffee pot, clean as the day it was new, filled it from the nearby bucket, and sat it on the steadily heating surface of the range.

"Feels so good," Laura said in a thankful voice. She leaned forward, extending her hands, palms outward, to the stove. "I'll never get used to this country! So hot in the day, yet it turns so bitterly cold at night."

He nodded. "Way of the desert." He squatted on his heels, began to roll a cigarette, doing it the quick deft way of a man who had performed the task a thousand times over. He lit the slim cylinder, sucked the smoke deeply into his lungs.

She watched him taking his ease for a time. There was calmness about him now, a quiet, relaxed quality to his sun-browned features that changed him, turned him into a different person. It was as if, within four walls, the world was far removed from his conscious self and there were no troubles, no threats, no promises of violence.

The water in the pot began to rumble, rattling the lid of the container. He rose, helped himself to a handful of already ground coffee, dumped it into the pot. The liquid boiled up immediately, and he pushed the granite utensil to the cooler side of the stove to simmer. He took two cups, dropped the oven door, improvising a convenient table, and placed them upon it. The room had grown warm and cheery.

He allowed the coffee to murmur for a bit. When he decided it was ready, he filled the cups. "This will hold us until the Lovelesses get up," he said. "Then we'll have some breakfast."

He went back to his haunches before the open oven, sipping at the black, steaming drink with relish. Laura finished her own portion, placing the cup aside on the edge of the stove. Automatically he reached for the granite pot.

She said: "Not just now."

He refilled his own, settling back again. She leaned toward him.

"What do you plan to do next, Ben?"

At her question he glanced up. "I want you to stay here with Abner and Hopeful. I'm going over to Diamond X and see what I can find out."

"Won't that be taking a big chance? Marr is sure to have everything watched."

Dunn shrugged. "No other answer that I can see. I've got to clear you, and myself, of that murder charge."

"What can you expect to learn there?"

"Several things. I want to talk to some of the old hands that worked for Pope. Mainly, though, I mean to get those things you mentioned, the ones that prove you are Isaac Pope's daughter. We've got to have them."

"They will be in the house, in his room, if they haven't been moved. Shouldn't I go with you and help?"

He said—"Too dangerous."—and ended the subject.

There was a sound behind them. They turned. Abner Loveless, clad in a long white nightgown, his thin hair askew, stood in the doorway of the bedroom. He saw Laura and hastily withdrew until only his head was visible.

"Thought I heard somethin' out here," he declared. "When'd you come, Ben?"

"Hour or so ago. This is Laura Pope, Isaac's daughter."

"Pleased to meet you," the old man said. He disappeared from sight. "Hopeful, get up!" he shouted into the bedroom. "We got us some company."

77

In a short time the old couple was dressed and gathered before the stove. Dunn poured them some coffee, making the introductions complete. When that was done, Hopeful Loveless, a sweet-faced woman with iron-gray hair, busied herself at her food stores.

" 'Spect you're mighty hungry. I'll get breakfast to cooking."

"I'll help," Laura volunteered, and moved to her side.

Abner Loveless placed his attention on Dunn. "Reckon you had reason for comin' here in the middle of the night. Anything I can do to help?"

Ben said: "Pope was killed last night."

"Kilt?" Loveless echoed, astonished. "Who by?"

"Marr is trying to put it on Laura and me. He's telling it around that we cooked up the deal so we could get our hands on the Diamond X."

Abner was silent for a long minute.

Dunn read the question that was in his mind. "She *is* Pope's daughter. She showed him proof and he accepted her before he was killed. I figure Jack Marr had a hand in it. He didn't want to lose out, so he got Pope out of the way before the old man could make it known that his daughter had come back."

"Then Jack started gunnin' for you two, figurin' he'd have to get you out of the way."

"He's got to hang it on somebody. Laura was the natural one. Then, me, too, because I helped her a little. We've been dodging Sabine and Frisco and the one they call Harvey all yesterday and last night."

"Where are they now?"

"Don't know exactly. Gave them the slip back on the mountain. They could have gone back to Pope's."

"Nope, they'll still be lookin'. What you figure to do next?"

"I'd like to leave Laura here with you. I'm riding over to Pope's to see what's going on and try to get my hands on that proof Laura needs before Jack destroys it."

"Be takin' quite a chance," Loveless said. "How you figure to get the stuff?"

"Something I don't know yet. Cross that creek when I get to it."

"Shame there ain't some law around here a man could turn to," Loveless muttered.

Laura heard his comment, came about. "I thought there was a marshal in Salt River!"

"A town marshal, miss," Abner explained. "He's got no authority outside Salt River, unless it's Jack Marr that's talkin' to him. Then he's as big as a United States marshal."

She faced Ben Dunn. "But if he . . . ?"

"Don't worry about it," he said. "If we get the proof we need, we'll convince him. But we've got to do it before Marr talks to him."

"What about the murder charge?"

Dunn shook his head. "Something I haven't figured out yet. Hope to get some idea of what happened when I get to Pope's. There's a few of the old hands still there that don't take much to Jack and his gun toughs. Might learn a few things from them."

"If you can get them to talk," Loveless amended.

"Something I've got to manage, somehow."

The meal was ready shortly after that. They gathered around the small table and ate in silence. When it was over, Dunn arose.

"Best I get started. I'd like to borrow one of your horses, Abner. That bay of mine is about run out."

"Sure," the old cowpuncher said. "I'll help you saddle up."

Ben turned to Laura. "Just wait here for me. It'll take most of the day, but I'll be back. You can figure on that."

She said: "All right."

"If anybody shows up, stay out of sight, no matter who it is. I don't want anybody carrying word to Marr or any of his bunch about there being a girl here. They would know right quick who it is."

Again she said: "All right." She moved a step nearer to him, looked up into his still face. "This is going to be dangerous for you, Ben. I'm not sure I want you to go. I'm not sure now that it's worth it. Isn't there some other way it can be done?"

"This is the only way I know," he said. "Don't fret about me. I've lived these many years, and I figure to keep on living a few more."

"You must . . . for my sake," she said softly. "Good bye."

"Good bye," he replied, and followed Abner Loveless out into the breaking dawn.

X

Ben Dunn lay on the top of the butte and studied the Pope ranch. The sun climbed steadily toward its midday peak, but activity below, for some obscure reason, seemed at a standstill. There were a number of horses, saddled and ready for use, waiting in the corral behind the bunkhouse. No one went near them. He saw three men emerge from their quarters, cross the yard to the main house. They entered only to reappear minutes later and stroll aimlessly to the barn and back. It was as though a holiday from all labor had been declared at the Diamond X.

This both mystified and dismayed Ben Dunn. To get the proof Laura needed to establish her claim and to search for facts that would enable him to clear them both of the murder charge, he had to get inside the ranch house. To accomplish this he had to wait until Jack Marr and his riders pulled out to go about the daily affairs. Today, however, something was amiss. Neither they nor any of the older hands were making any move to depart.

He laid sprawled full length on the rim of the lava butte and puzzled over the matter. It was while he was thus engrossed that he caught the sounds of an approaching horse. It came from the east, from the general direction of Comanche Mountain. He threw a quick glance to his own mount, picketed a dozen yards down the slope. Growth along the black, ragged formation was scant. There was little he could do to conceal the animal's presence from anyone arriving on that side. But he could provide himself with some degree of cover. He rolled swiftly to a nearby clump of stringy greasewood. It made a poor screen, but it would afford him the chance to see who the oncoming rider might be.

It was Laura Pope. Her name leaped from his lips when her worn horse broke out of a narrow arroyo, pulled up onto the top of the butte. She halted instantly. A wave of fear washed over her features when she heard his exclamation, but it disappeared at once when she recognized him. She smiled.

"Stay there!" he called.

He worked his way back from the edge of the butte until he reached a point where he would not be seen by anyone at the ranch, and, then rising, he hurried to her.

She was near exhaustion. He reached for her and lifted her from the saddle, noting as he did so that she was riding a Diamond X horse. He carried her to a shallow basin where a twisted juniper had managed to grow. He laid her in its dappled shade.

"I'm so glad I found you," she said. "I didn't think it was so far."

He dropped back to his horse, obtained his canteen. Returning, he poured a little of the tepid water between her lips. He wet his fingers and dampened her forehead and temples.

She smiled up at him. "I feel better."

She had pulled on an old, faded pair of Abner's denims over her dress and had covered her shoulders with one of his light jackets. The hat she wore to protect her head from the driving sun was one of Hopeful's. He set aside the canteen.

"What happened back at the Loveless place? Why did you come here?"

"It was those men who were after us. Sabine and the

other two. They came an hour or so after you had left. We saw them in time, and Abner hid me out in a shed, after furnishing me with these clothes. He was afraid they would search the place and told me, if they did, I was to leave at once. We arranged a signal and he showed me the trail I was to take that would lead me to you, or where he figured you would be. They came, tied their horses up to the corral only a few feet from where I was hiding. When Abner gave me the signal, I took the first horse I could get to . . . one of theirs . . . and lit out."

Dunn thought for a few moments. "I'm glad you managed to get away," he said finally. "Did you hear any shooting back at Abner's?"

"No, but when I looked back later, I saw a lot of smoke. I guess they burned down their house."

Dunn stared off into the east. His jaw was set to grim, hard lines. "If they hurt those people," he said in a voice so low she could scarcely hear, "they'll answer to me. I've tried to avoid any bloodshed, but they'll have it if they've done anything bad to the Lovelesses."

"I thought later, when I was coming here, that maybe I should have stayed. Perhaps I could have helped."

He shook his head. "No. Abner was right. Finding you there would have made things worse. The lucky part is that you found me."

"Abner pointed to a gap in the hills. Said you would be going into it. Is the ranch near here?"

"Just below this butte," he said. "I've been watching but still haven't figured out how to get inside the house. Seems everybody's hanging around close."

Laura came to a sitting position. "Don't try it, Ben," she said earnestly. "After you left this morning, I was sorry I let you go. I don't care about the Diamond X any more. Let

Jack Marr have it. I realized that all that mattered to me is you."

He glanced at her briefly. His arm went quickly about her, and he drew her swiftly to him. "Hearing you say that means a lot to me, everything, in fact. But I wouldn't let myself hope too much. Pretty poor sort of a life is all I can offer you."

"All I want. Just the two of us together . . . to be left in peace."

He was silent for a time. Then: "Wish it could be that easy. You forget Marr. He'll never let it lie. We're a threat to him, long as we're alive."

"Why?" she wondered, drawing back from him. "If I give up my claim on the Diamond X, why wouldn't he forget about us?"

"Man like him has to be sure of his ground. He could never be. And then there's the death of your father to be accounted for. He's branded us as the killers. We have to clear that up for our own sake."

"Can't we just go away, leave this country, and start over somewhere else where nobody knows us?"

"Running away won't be the answer," he said. "I learned that a long time ago."

"What can we do then? You can't fight them all!"

"We've got to get inside the house," he replied. "We need the proof that will back your claim to being Isaac Pope's daughter. That will knock apart Marr's contention that you are an imposter. When that's done, it'll be a big step toward making him eat that murder charge."

"That proof won't be hard to find," she said, "if Marr hasn't already destroyed it. Some of it he may not have known about. The tintypes my father said were in a trunk, for instance. And there was that box of papers by the bed."

"Only way we're going to know for sure about anything is to get inside the house and look. You feel all right now?"

She nodded. "What do we do next?"

"Go back to the rim and watch the ranch. Soon as Marr and his bunch leave, we'll go down. We'll have to take a chance on the regular help."

They crawled back to the lip of the butte, looking down upon the Pope buildings. They were scarcely settled when the side door opened and a man came out. He walked quickly to the barn and disappeared into it for a short time. He reappeared driving a light wagon. He guided it to the front of the house and halted.

Minutes later several men walked out onto the gallery, taking up positions in the yard beyond the vehicle. Immediately they were followed by six others carrying a coffin between them. As they moved to the wagon, slid the elongated box onto its bed, Dunn realized why there had been no activity around the ranch during the early hours. They were holding a funeral for Isaac Pope.

More persons came from the house, lined up in pairs behind the wagon. Other than the man who appeared to be a minister, it looked as though no outsiders and only those who worked for the Diamond X were attending the burial.

The procession began, headed out across the yard for the small, family cemetery on a slight rise of ground a half mile distant. Ben felt Laura stir at his side. He placed his hand upon hers.

"I know I should be sad," she said. "He was my father. But I never knew him. I remember seeing him only that once, when I came the other day."

"Nobody would expect more of you," Dunn assured her. "I didn't know him, either. Met him only a couple of times. He was a hard man, tough as they come, but he was honest

85

and he was fair. Expect that's as good a recommendation as any man could have."

The long cortège was fully strung out by then. It appeared all of Diamond X's hands were in it, even the Mexican cook who walked along by herself.

"This is going to be our chance," Dunn said. "They'll be gone an hour, at least. Gives us time to reach the house, find the things we need and get out."

She said: "I'm ready when you are."

"Be better if you wait here. No use for you to take any risk."

"No, I want to be with you, Ben. Besides, I know where everything is. We can save time if I go. How do we get off this bluff?"

He grinned at her. She could be determined when she wished. He pointed off to their left. "There's a break in the butte a couple of hundred yards. We can ride down, cross over, and come in behind the ranch house. That patch of trees will be a good place to leave the horses."

She began to withdraw from the rim. "We should get started. I'd hate to get trapped inside the house."

XI

It required no more than a quarter hour to descend from the butte and reach the house. They hid their horses in the trees, crossed quickly to the front door of the low, rambling structure, and let themselves in. It would be better to use that particular entrance, Dunn reasoned, for, if there were some who had not joined the cortège, they most likely would be somewhere in the rear of the building.

Once inside, he locked the door and secured it behind them. The house was hot, stuffy, and heavy with a silence that was at once oppressive. They stood quietly and listened for any sounds that would indicate there were others about, but heard nothing.

Dunn said: "Expect we'd better get busy. We'll try Pope's room first."

They crossed the cluttered parlor, went down the hallway to where he had last seen Isaac Pope alive. The door was closed. He turned the knob softly, pushed the panel wide. The rancher's sleeping quarters were just as he had last seen them, with the exception of the now empty bed.

"That box you mentioned . . . where was it?"

Laura said—"In the top drawer of that washstand."—and pointed to the dark, varnished piece of furniture against the wall.

Dunn stepped to it, pulled open the designated drawer. It was empty. Quickly he went through the rest. Except for some odds and ends of clothing, there was nothing of interest. He turned then to the bed itself, giving it a thorough search. There was no box. They went through the remainder of the room, finding nothing. It was evident that the metal container Laura had seen Isaac Pope refer to had been removed.

"Where did you leave your bag?" Dunn asked.

She turned almost immediately, leading the way to the bedroom she had used. A complete examination of it revealed that her small carpetbag, with its papers, was also missing. In the deathly quiet house, they paused.

"It's no use," she said in a falling voice. "Marr has already taken care of everything."

Dunn shrugged. He crossed to a window where he could look out into the yard. He looked to the north, to the direction in which the funeral procession had disappeared. There was no one in sight. He pivoted slowly to Laura.

"Did Pope have an office or a room where he kept his records? Might be a desk there. And that trunk."

"I don't know," she answered. "There are several more rooms down that hall. One that Marr used."

They started along the corridor. At the first door, Dunn halted. He opened the darkly stained panel. It was another bedroom. He went through it hurriedly, found nothing of interest.

"Marr's room," he said, rejoining Laura in the hall. "I hardly expected to find any of the things we're looking for in there. He would have hidden them some other place."

They moved on to the next door. It proved to be a storage closet containing only bedding. There was one more opening in the corridor before it turned to a right angle and led to the rear of the house.

"This should be it," Dunn said, and reached for the knob.

Somewhere a door slammed. Ben's hand, resting on the

round contour of the handle, froze. At his shoulder, Laura drew up sharply. A gasp escaped her lips.

"Somebody is here," she whispered in a strained voice.

He frowned, cautioning her to silence. Touching her lightly on the arm, he motioned for her to remain where she stood. He glided off then into the short stretch of hallway to his right, which, if he were guessing right, led to the dining quarters and the kitchen. He could not tell where the sound of the closing door had come from. He was certain it had not been in the front of the house.

The hall led out into the mess hall, as he had anticipated. He halted there in the open doorway, glancing about. The room was deserted. Through a bank of windows on the opposite side he could look into the yard, see the rear of the bunkhouse, the front of the barn. There was no one in sight. He brought his attention back to the dining area. To his left, at the end of the narrow room, was a door. He walked quickly to it, opening it softly, slowly. It was the kitchen. It, too, was forsaken.

Puzzled, he remained there, alert, listening. He heard only the distant, raucous scolding of a crow in the field beyond the barn. But a door had slammed—somewhere. He became aware of the fleeting moments. He could waste no more time searching for it. They would just have to gamble that the sound had come from outside, from one of the other buildings. He wheeled, retracing his steps to Laura. To her questioning glance, he shook his head.

"Somewhere in the yard, I reckon."

He opened the door before them. It was Isaac Pope's office, or what had served for such. A huge, roll-top desk stood against one wall. Near it was a metal-bound, domed-lid trunk that showed evidence of much usage. Ben went straight to it, Laura close at his side.

"He said something about pictures," she recalled.

Dunn immediately began to delve through it. After a time he straightened up. In his hands was a large, family Bible. He opened it, quickly read the finely scripted words on the first sheet.

"The record," he said. "Shows here there was a daughter. Now all we need is something to prove you are that daughter."

With Laura peering over his shoulder, he hastily leafed through the thick book, coming finally to several pages in the back into which had been inserted, in squares and ovals provided for them, a number of tintype photographs.

"Here it is," he announced. "Here's what we need."

There was the wedding picture of Pope and the woman that was his wife.

"My mother," Laura murmured.

Below it was a date. There were two other likenesses of persons unknown, and then one of a small child with flowing, dark curls and large eyes.

"That must be you," he said.

On the next page they found more of what they needed. There was a picture of Pope with his wife and their small daughter, one of Pope holding Laura on his knee, and a third of her in the arms of her mother.

"That's the picture I have . . . or had . . . the one my mother gave me," Laura stated. "Or rather, one just like it. That should be all we need to show the marshal."

Dunn said: "Maybe. We still have to prove to the marshal that you're the same girl."

"But the picture I have," Laura began, and then faltered. "I forgot. It was in my bag."

"Exactly. We've got to find that bag. With the picture

you have and the letter your mother wrote, we've got this thing licked."

He turned to Pope's desk, went through each pigeonhole and drawer, coming up with nothing of value. "Let's take a look through the parlor," he said, and went back into the hallway. "Hardly a place where Marr would hide something, but it's our last bet."

They fell to the task at once, systematically checking every drawer, every shelf, all possible places. Eventually they gave it up.

"Either it isn't hidden inside the house or Marr has destroyed it," Dunn said.

Laura, her face solemn, said: "Could it be in the bunkhouse?"

Ben considered that. "Don't think so. Like the kitchen and the mess hall, I don't think he'd risk hiding it there. Too much chance of someone else finding it."

She moved up to him. "What can we do, Ben?"

He put his arm around her. "Don't worry, we're not licked yet. It's possible he's got it with him, carrying it in his saddlebags and waiting for a good moment to get rid of it." He stopped, adding: "Wonder if we've got time to check in the barn and have a look at Marr's gear?"

He stepped away abruptly, glanced out the window. "Too late," he said. "They're coming back. We've got to get out of here."

Laura ran to his side. Several men were just beginning the descent of the low rise to the north. Others, strung out irregularly, trailed them. Ben picked up the Bible, tucked it under his arm.

"We've got this much, anyway. And it might do the trick."

"But the one who did it . . . who killed my father . . . we

haven't been able to find out anything about that!"

"That will have to come later."

There was the sudden drum of trotting horses outside in the yard. Dunn wheeled, threw his attention to that point.

"Who is it?" Laura asked, pressing close to him.

"Sabine," he answered, "with Frisco and Harvey. Guess they're just getting back from the Loveless place. That's one of Abner's horses Frisco is riding."

"Someone else is coming," Laura said. "Another man."

Dunn bent down to follow her direction, looked under the partly drawn shade. Sabine and the two riders with him had stopped and awaited the newcomer. Dunn, suddenly tense, straightened up slowly.

Laura saw the change sweep over him. She said: "Who is it? Do you know him?"

He did not immediately answer. Then—"I know him."—he said in a quiet voice. "That's Jay Greavey."

XII

"Greavey!" Laura Pope echoed the name as though it were the foreboding of doomsday. She clutched at Dunn's arm. "He's that man . . . that killer . . . you've been expecting to come?"

He did not answer. For him, that moment was like taking a long step back into the years that had gone. In the past few days he had been a different man, one living in a newly born world in which there had been no shadows, one for whom there had been only the present and the future. His thoughts had centered on Laura, on what lay ahead for them. Now suddenly, in the shape of an almost frail-looking man with sloped shoulders, a narrow face, and flat, colorless eyes, the old world he had left behind once again possessed him.

His hand dropped to the gun at his hip, touched its smooth, worn butt. A coolness enveloped him, seeped into his long body, steadied his nerves. He threw a glance to the ridge. Marr and the other Diamond X people were in sight. Their advance was slow, but they would not be long in reaching the yard. He calculated the risk. With three of Marr's men already at hand and the remainder only a short distance away, he would have no chance, even if he were to down Greavey at first clash. Besides, there was Laura to consider.

Through the window he heard Bibo Sabine say: "You lookin' for somebody, mister?"

Greavey said: "I am. Man by the name of Dunn. Heard he was living around in these parts. He work for this outfit?"

"Who's askin'?" Sabine's words were blunt, too blunt.

"Don't see as that's any of your business. But the name happens to be Greavey. Dunn here?"

Sabine shook his head. "Don't work here but I reckon I know him, all right. Better you wait for the boss. That's him comin' over there."

The gunman astride a tall sorrel swung his narrow visage toward the ridge at which Sabine pointed. The horse was a nervous animal and continually fiddled his hoofs, backed, and shied. Greavey jerked at the reins. "Damn horse is just new broke. What's been going on? A burying?"

"Just that," Sabine said. "This here Dunn you're talkin' about stuck a knife in the owner of this ranch. If you're a friend of his'n. . . ."

"I'm not," Greavey said shortly.

"Ben," Laura broke into Dunn's consciousness. "What are we going to do?"

Her question brought an awareness of their immediate peril. He wheeled about. "We're getting out of here," he said, and started across the room.

There was no escape through the front door or out of the kitchen. With Laura at his heels, he moved down the hallway, entering Pope's quarters. He crossed the small room quickly to one of the windows, raised it fully. The screen was nailed shut. He whipped out his knife, slashed the light wire mesh.

"Quick," he said to the girl.

He helped her through the opening, followed himself. He closed the window, but there was nothing he could do about the sagging screen. It did not matter too much. They were on the side of the house, opposite to the yard.

They broke into a run, crossing the open ground to where their horses waited. He helped Laura into the saddle, and then swung up himself.

"Keep to the brush," he said, pulling the bay around him. They moved out, holding their mounts to a walk. Dunn, one hand impeded by the Pope family Bible, twisted about, secured the book to his saddle with the leather strips provided for such purpose. Likely he would be needing both hands before the hour was over.

The narrow band of green cover began to thin out, resolving itself into short clumps of brush. At its end, Dunn halted. He turned about, looked toward the Pope ranch. Marr and the others had returned. He could not see the man himself, but the others were visible, moving around in that area behind the ranch house and in front of the barn and corral. Four riders waited in the saddle, apparently for Marr. Ben was not certain but he thought one was Greavey.

He brought his attention back to their own present situation. Ahead lay a long mile of almost smooth, barren country before they could reach the first outcropping of trees and brush that trickled down from the mountain. To their right, the lava buttes were an equal distance away, offering even less protection. He considered for a time, came to a decision.

"Can't stay here. We'll try for those trees straight ahead." Laura smiled. If she were aware of the danger that lay ahead of them, when they broke out into the open, she did not show it.

"Get in front of me," he said, and pulled off to one side. "We may make it without being separated, and, if we do, ride straight up the side of the mountain."

"If we get separated . . . ?" she began haltingly.

"Don't stop. Try to get as far up the slope as you can. I'll find you. Ready?"

"Ready," she said, and pushed on by him.

Her horse, or that of Pete Frisco, was tired. He wouldn't go far at a fast pace, Dunn saw. But they had no choice. And it was wiser to keep the better mount under him. If it became necessary, he could draw Marr and his riders off, allowing Laura to escape.

Detection came quickly, even sooner than he had anticipated. They were no more than a hundred yards away from cover when he looked back, saw half a dozen riders streaming out of the yard in pursuit. He glanced ahead. It was a long way to the trees, but, barring any accident, they would make it. Their lead on the Diamond X riders was of sufficient length to make it possible.

He swung his attention back to the riders again. *Was Jay Greavey with them?* he wondered, but at such distance he could not tell.

It was a close race, nearer than he had thought it would be. They reached the first scatter of brush and trees with Marr and the others little more than a hundred yards behind. He pulled up to Laura's side.

"Keep going!" he shouted. "I'll cut off, try to lead them away."

He did not wait for her to answer, simply veered his horse sharply left, heading into the steadily thickening forest. He heard a yell go up as he purposely exposed himself, knew at once they had risen to the bait. He cast a glance to the direction in which Laura had gone. She was already out of sight, swallowed up by the maze of rock and green growth.

He let the bay have his head, allowed him to rush on down the lanes between the pines and other trees. Guns opened up a short time later, but he heard no droning of bullets and guessed the men were shooting wildly, hoping only to get lucky.

The forest grew denser, began to slow the horse down considerably. Rocks and huge boulders were becoming more plentiful. Dunn realized he was driving into the heart of a rough area, a place where once a massive slide had occurred. This suited him well.

At the first opportunity, at a narrow ravine, he cut to his right, doubling back at a slight climb. He reached a small pocket in the rain-washed rocks, halted. There he was effectively screened from the lower level by piles of rock. He remained still, listening. In only moments he heard the thunder of Marr and his riders hurrying by. They had passed up the rugged slide area, guessing that he would continue on through the easier-traveled forest.

Satisfied with the turn of the chase, he put the bay into motion, striking out for the higher slopes of the mountain. He would find Laura. They would remain in hiding until Marr tired of the hunt and gave it up. They could then decide what next was to be done.

He located the girl an hour later. Moving silently through the trees, on a higher plane where pine needles and oak leaves cushioned the floor of the forest, he saw first a patch of her dress which was exposed beneath the jacket she wore. He headed for it. Rounding a thick stand of brush, he came upon her, sitting on a fallen log at the edge of an arroyo. Pete Frisco's horse, near exhaustion, stood a few yards away, head down, legs spread in the way of a spent animal.

She sprang to her feet as he came up, greeted him with a glad, relieved smile. "I heard all that shooting. I was afraid. . . ."

"They didn't see me," he explained, and swung down. "They were just shooting wild, hoping they'd make a hit. Are you all right?"

She moved up to him, put herself in the circle of his arms. "I'm fine," she murmured. "And I'm glad you're all right. When we're apart, I worry so. I'm always afraid I won't see you again. . . ."

"Just stand easy!" a voice in the brush ordered. "My gun's on you, Dunn."

Ben stiffened. Greavey's voice! He felt Laura go tense against his body and begin to tremble. He swore inwardly. He had misjudged the gunman. Greavey had been smart enough to keep his eyes on Laura, knowing that Dunn would return to her if he managed to elude Marr. Grimfaced, he watched Greavey ride from the brush. The big sorrel stepped gingerly through the rocks and low brush.

"Get away from him, lady."

Ben pushed Laura to one side, until she was an arm's length away. She was staring at the gunman with a sort of fascination, her eyes spread wide with fear and horror. Dunn felt Greavey's empty gaze upon him, hard-cored and drilling.

"Been a long time," the gunman said in his soft, flat voice. "You sure dropped out of sight good." He jerked savagely at his reins, sought to settle down the nervous sorrel.

Dunn made no answer to his comments, simply rode out the long, terrible moments. That Greavey would give him his chance to use his own gun, of that he was certain. But that would come later, after Greavey played his game of cat and mouse. It was the way of gunslingers.

"Rode myself across this country half a dozen times. Never could find you. You been hiding in a hole?"

"Not hardly," Dunn said. "Got a ranch of my own now. Been there ever since I quit riding. Reckon you never came this way."

"Guess that's the truth," Greavey said. "Figured you'd

be over Texas way." He paused to check the sorrel which was attempting to wheel completely around. He halted the horse. "Heard about you in Santa Fé. Never knew you hankered to be a cattle raiser. You should've took it up before you went after my brother. Then you could have kept on growing your cows."

"Your brother was a job I had to do," Dunn said coldly. "Same as all the others."

"One time you picked the wrong job," Greavey said. "Anyway, it don't change nothing. He's still dead and you're the man that killed him. Leaves it all up to me."

"No point to it," Dunn said. "It's a long time gone. If I kill you here, today, or you kill me, what's gained?"

Greavey's pale eyes narrowed. "What gives you the idea that you'll be getting any chance at me?"

Dunn shrugged. "I know you, Jay. And all your kind. I'll have my chance to draw. One thing you've got to find out is whether you're faster than me. If you just shot me down, you'd always wonder about it. And wondering about something like that eats away at a man like you."

"You're mighty cocksure," Greavey said. "Been a few years since you done your bounty hunting."

"But I kept my hand in. I've been expecting you. Knew you'd show, sooner or later."

"No! No!" Laura cried suddenly and flung herself on Dunn.

He caught her in his arms, gently pushing her aside for the second time. At her unexpected movement, Greavey's sorrel shied violently, almost fell.

Dunn faced the gunman. "There's no call for this," he said when the horse had quieted down. "But if you will have it, let's get on with it."

Greavey said: "Fine. Just you stand quiet. Soon as I get

on the ground, I'll holster my iron and we'll start from scratch."

Dunn only nodded. He wished there was some way he could persuade Laura to leave, but knew it was useless to try. He watched Greavey, gun still in hand and leveled at him, shift his weight to his left and prepare to dismount. At that change, the skittish animal danced off to the right and began to back.

"Whoa!" Greavey yelled. "Whoa, damn you!"

The sorrel suddenly was on the rim of the arroyo. His right rear hoof missed the edge, pawing frantically in the air. Abruptly he was off balance, began scrambling for footing.

Greavey shouted another curse at the thoroughly frightened animal. He brought his weapon about in a swift arc, endeavoring to aim it at Dunn. Loose rock and earth broke out from under the frantic horse. He started to fall, threshing wildly. Greavey fired, determined to settle with Dunn in any event. The bullet went high, passing well above Dunn's head, as the gunman and the sorrel slipped over backward into the ravine.

XIII

Ben Dunn reacted quickly. He drew his pistol, stepped to the edge of the arroyo. The sorrel was struggling to his feet. The whites of his eyes mirrored his fright and his jaws slavered froth. Beyond him lay Jay Greavey. He was spread-eagled on the ground, his gun half buried in the sand where it had fallen. His head had struck a stone. Either he was dead or unconscious.

Dunn looked down upon the man who was determined to kill him. It could end there. With a single bullet he could close a door to the past, eliminate forever, perhaps, the possibility of trouble arising to haunt him again. He studied the senseless Greavey for a long minute, and then with a shrug he slid his revolver into his holster and wheeled about.

Laura had been watching him. He saw relief spread over her features, knew she had read the thoughts that had passed through his mind. She was glad of his decision. She ran to him, threw her arms about him, and for a time they were locked in an embrace. Finally he took her shoulders between his broad hands, holding her at arm's length.

"We can't stay here. It's not safe. Marr and his bunch are somewhere close. And Greavey won't sleep long."

"Where can we go?"

"Farther up the mountain. We can watch better from there. Soon as it's safe, we'll move on. It's going to be a race from here on."

"To Salt River?"

"That's it," he answered. "We've got enough proof now, I think, to back our story. Anyway, we'll try it on the marshal. If he won't listen, we'll telegraph the United States marshal in El Paso. I know him."

They turned, took up the reins of their horses, and, on foot, started along the edge of the ravine. They came to a break in the wall, dropped down into the sandy depth, crossed over and gained the opposite side. There they swung to the saddle and, favoring their mounts, began to ascend the long slope.

The day was growing on to noon. Heat and thirst were beginning to make themselves felt. There was a canteen on Pete Frisco's saddle, but it was empty. It would remain so, for they were heading away from the spring, and there was not another on that side of Comanche Mountain.

Behind him, Dunn heard Laura ask: "What will that Greavey do when he comes to? Will he . . . ?"

"Look for me?" Ben supplied the words. "Sure. He'll just start over again. Might join up with Marr, or he could try to pick up our trail on his own."

"Oh." The word was a complete expression of her disappointment. "I thought that maybe, when he sees that you didn't go ahead and kill him while he was lying there, he would be grateful enough to ride on and forget about you."

Ben shook his head. "Not Greavey, or any of his kind. Sure, he'll be grateful, but not that much. He'll figure he owes me a favor, but it won't change what he thinks he has to do."

A sob wrenched from her lips. "I almost wish you had gone ahead and killed him when you had the chance. All this terrible hunting and shooting and killing . . . it's not human!"

He dropped back to her side. "Maybe," he said. "But I couldn't have done it. It would have been cold-blooded murder. No matter who Greavey is or what he figures to do to me, I couldn't do it. And you wouldn't have wanted me to."

"I know," she murmured. "I just forgot myself for a moment. Oh, Ben, I'm about at my wit's end! I don't think I can stand much more of this."

"You won't need to," he replied. "This time tomorrow, you'll be safe in Salt River."

The slope had begun to become steeper, forcing the horses to labor. Dunn halted, came down from the saddle. He helped Laura do the same.

"Better give these horses a breather. I should have borrowed that sorrel of Greavey's and left him this horse of Pete Frisco's. He's about done for."

Laura said nothing. She sank down in the narrow shade of a lightning-blasted stump. "Can we rest here for a little?"

"Better place higher up," he said. "A ledge where we can watch below for quite a ways. We've got to be on the lookout for Marr and the others. It's only a short walk."

She said: "I'm so tired. Seems like weeks since I had any sleep."

"Once we're on the ledge, you can have your sleep," he promised.

They resumed the climb, still leading the bay and Frisco's spent buckskin. Soon they broke out into a small clearing beneath the hogback. It was too steep at that point to scale, and they cut left, following along the base of the rock ledge until it faded into the body of the mountain itself. From there it was fairly simple to quarter the slope and drop back upon the shelf.

Ben led the way to its widest point, to where it jutted out at its farthest, and there they stopped. He picketed the horses back in the trees, where there was grazing to be had, and returned to Laura. He raked up a quantity of dead leaves and pine needles, shaped up a bed for her in the shade of a towering spruce. She thanked him, crawling into it at once. He kissed her lightly and moved to the edge of the ridge to take up his post. She was asleep before he had settled himself.

Midday wore by. The after hours, hot and hushed, began. From time to time, he dozed, cat-like, taking his rest as he could but never for more than a few minutes at one length. He kept a sharp surveillance on the slope and the level ground far below, watching for Jay Greavey, or Marr's party sweeping back in an all-out search.

He could think of nothing better than going on to Salt River and endeavoring to enlist the aid of the law, in one form or another. He could see no point in doubling back to the Loveless place. He had involved them too deeply now, and to call on them again for any help would only bring them more trouble. He hoped Sabine and his two companions had not done the couple any bodily harm. He could help them rebuild their house and sheds, but there was nothing he could do toward shouldering any suffering—except take revenge.

Getting to Salt River would be no easy chore. They first must have a canteen of water, and then some food. And a horse for Laura. His own bay likely could make the trip if not pressed too hard, but the buckskin that had been Pete Frisco's was out of the question. He cursed himself silently again for not swapping mounts with Jay Greavey when he had had the opportunity.

There was one answer—swing over to his own place. There he could obtain food and water and a fresh horse for the girl. He could even exchange the one he rode.

The problem and course of action settled in his mind, he lay back, continued to rest and maintain his vigil. When the sun reached its mid-afternoon position, he arose, went to where Laura slept. He shook her gently.

She sat up instantly, alarmed. "Is there trouble?"

He said: "No. Just time to leave."

He moved on by her to where the horses waited. He took up the reins, led them to the ledge. "We'll go to my ranch first," he said, helping her mount. While she settled herself, he explained the plan.

She felt much better for her rest and showed it. "Are we far from there?"

"Couple of hours," he replied, and swung onto his bay. "Not a lot of miles but rough going most of the way. We have to take it slow."

They kept fairly high on the side of Comanche Mountain. There was no trail, only the unmarked slope. There were times when they were forced to drop lower or climb higher to circumvent an impassable outcropping of rock or some deep, storm-gouged cañon.

Eventually they were in more familiar surroundings, and Ben Dunn sought out the less arduous routes but never forsook an alert vigilance for comfort. They reached the southernmost boundary of his property and there started a gradual descent, working their way downward to level ground.

Abruptly Dunn pulled to a halt.

"What is it?" Laura asked, moving quickly to his side. "Did you hear something?"

He shook his head. "No, I thought I smelled smoke." A frown creased his face. His jaw settled into a hard angle. "Come on. We're close so we'll have to go quiet. Might be someone around."

He feared that less than he did the persistent suspicion that now crowded his mind. Minutes later, when they

halted at the edge of the clearing in which his ranch buildings sat, he saw that what he had feared had come true. His
house, his small barn, all that he owned were little more
than charred, smoking embers. The Box B had been burned
to the ground. And there were no horses.

XIV

For a long time he sat in absolute silence staring at the ruins. All he had worked for was gone. All he owned, except for the clothing on his back, the stock and the land itself, had been ruthlessly taken from him.

"Three years," he murmured, "down a hole."

He felt Laura touch his arm, heard her say: "Ben, I'm sorry. I feel it's my fault. If I hadn't dragged you into this, it never would have happened."

His dark face was set. "Maybe . . . and maybe not. I know Jack Marr's kind. This whole country wouldn't be big enough for him, once he got the fever to grab, and grow. Someday he would have found another excuse."

"It must have been Sabine and those other two men. Probably did this when they came back from the Loveless place. The fire has been out for some time."

He agreed. But he was not thinking so much of his loss, now that the initial shock was over, as he was of their immediate circumstance. Without at least one fresh horse, the journey to Salt River was out of the question, and they could not remain here. Marr and his crew would be searching for them on one hand, the flat-eyed gunman, Jay Greavey, on the other.

"Wait here," he said. "I'll have a look around."

He pulled the bay about, faded off into the brush. There was a chance, a slim one, that his horses were close by. He recalled that Sabine and his two friends had ridden into the Diamond X with no extra mounts, that Pete Frisco had been astride a horse he had taken from Abner Loveless. It was possible, he reasoned, that they had simply hazed the animals out of the barn and driven them off into the forest.

After several minutes' search, he failed to turn up any of them. Disappointed, he circled back to Laura, after assuring himself there was no one else lurking nearby. Rejoining her, he again looked over his desolate buildings. The well had been spared, he noted. Even men such as Bibo Sabine hesitated to destroy, in any way, that priceless necessity in the West—water.

"Guess we can still get a drink," he said, and led the way around the charred remains to the small housing that sheltered the well. They dismounted and secured the horses. He dropped the bucket down the narrow shaft, reeled it up. He served Laura. When she finished, he satisfied his own thirst, and then provided for the two horses. While they drank greedily, he walked out into the center of the blackened ruins.

Squares of stone marked the foundations upon which his three rooms had rested. In the ashes he saw the remnants of a few possessions: the misshapen, blackened pot and pans, the kitchen stove. There lay the barrel of his shotgun with the wooden stock burned away, the skeleton of his other pistol.

He kicked it with the toe of his boot, reached down, and picked it up. Here was the gun that had driven him there, he thought bitterly. Now it would be one like it, the so carefully matched mate, that would take him away—perhaps forever. He had no illusions as to what lay ahead. If it were only Jay Greavey that was to be faced, it would be a different matter. But Jack Marr, with half a dozen gunslingers at his side, was something else.

His one hope was that Jay Greavey would stay clear of it, would not show up to prevent his squaring accounts with the Diamond X crew. He needed to do that, not only for himself but for Laura, as well. If there was nothing to be salvaged of his own life, he could at least help her. That was just what he would be doing if he erased Marr from the picture.

He should be taking steps to insure that. Marr would be back, he was certain. They would come looking for him there, sooner or later. This time they would find him, ready and waiting. He wheeled, walking back slowly to the well where Laura waited in silence. He unhooked the canteen from Frisco's saddle, filled it. Tightening the cap, he hung it on the bay.

He squatted down before Laura, picked up a twig. "Look, I'll show you how to reach Salt River."

She dropped to his side. "Salt River?" she echoed, her voice rising with surprise. "I thought we were going together!"

"There's only one horse that can make it. You take him. I'll hang around here until I can get my hands on another. Then I'll follow."

She frankly distrusted his words. "Another? Where will you get another horse?"

He shrugged. "Figure there's a chance one of mine will come wandering back. Horses sometimes do that along about dark."

"Then why can't I just wait?"

"I said it was just a chance. Could be tomorrow or the next day before I'll find one. Best you get started right away." He drew a square in the moist earth. "Here's where we are now. And here's the mountain. You head out south on the trail and follow it until you are on the other side of the mountain. The trail forks there. Take the right hand and it will lead you to Salt River. Understand?"

109

She said: "Yes, but I don't want to go and leave you."

"Only thing to do," he said. "Anyway, quick as I get a horse, I'll follow. Like to catch up to you before you've gone halfway."

He reached into his pocket, drew forth several coins. He handed them to her. "This will get you a room at the hotel and buy you meals at the restaurant." He paused, scratched in the soft earth with the stick. "Come to think of it, when you get there, go first to that lawyer who's got an office next to the bank. Can't recall his name but he knows me. I had him draw up some papers for me once. You tell him what's happened and that I sent you to him. Show him that Bible and the things we found in it. Tell him what you're up against."

"And I shouldn't go to the marshal?"

"Let him decide that. I figure you're better off to talk to him first, just in case Marr has already sent word to the marshal. He'll know what's best to do."

"You'll come as soon as you can?"

"Soon as I can," he said. "Don't push the bay too hard and he'll make it. You won't have to run him. I'll see that nobody follows you."

She looked at him more closely. A frown darkened her features. "You are expecting more trouble, aren't you? And one reason you're staying behind is so I can go free."

"We've got just one horse," he reminded her. "If we had another that could make it, I'd be right with you."

"I still think I should wait for you. . . ."

He rose to his feet. "Do as I say," he said in a firm but gentle voice. "I know what I'm doing. You had better get started. Be dark in a couple of hours." He turned to where the bay waited, pulled loose the reins. "Remember, don't crowd your horse and he'll be all right. Sure you got the directions right?"

"I'm sure," she murmured, and moved up to him. She reached out, pulled his head down to a level with hers, kissed him fully on the lips. "Don't be too long in coming. I won't rest easy until I see you again."

He grinned. "You just get to Salt River and that lawyer. That's all you need worry about."

"I don't want the ranch," she said, "not unless I can be with you. I'd rather give it up. . . ."

Her words trailed off, faded from his consciousness. Movement in the brush beyond the clearing halted his awareness of all else. His eyes swung about in a brief circle. There were riders—Diamond X riders—all around them, encircling them. It was suddenly too late for all things.

XV

Jack Marr, Pete Frisco, Bibo Sabine—a dozen others. They were there, every last one of them. They had eased about, now enclosing them in a silent, almost complete circle. Marr rode forward a dozen paces. Frisco and Sabine flanked him. Marr glanced casually at the blackened remains of the Box B.

"Boys did a right good job here, don't you think so, Dunn?"

Ben made no reply. A wild hate was tearing at his insides, flaring through his eyes. He moved a slow step away from Laura. Jack Marr was a dead man, whether he knew it or not. Sabine and Frisco would get in their shots, but not before he blasted the sneering Marr from his saddle.

"Knew you'd show up here again," Marr said. "Told the boys so. You're not very smart, mister."

Dunn remained silent, still not trusting himself much. In the hush that followed Marr's words, one of the horses shifted his weight, blew noisily. Leather creaked in its dry way. Tension suddenly was a tangible element, evident as the sky itself. Through it Ben Dunn was desperately seeking to come up with an answer to a new problem that now faced him—how to get Laura safely free and away from the inevitable showdown that was coming?

"Tell me something, Dunn," Marr said, slouching to one side of his saddle, "did you actually think you and your woman could get away with it?"

"We weren't trying to get away with anything!" Laura exclaimed, finding her voice. "You know that! And we aren't guilty of doing anything wrong!"

Marr laughed. That sound was immediately taken up and echoed by Sabine and Frisco.

"I'll say this," Marr observed in mock admiration, "you're a hard one to put off, lady. And a cool one. You'd have to be to stick a knife in an old, sick man."

"That's a lie!" Dunn snapped. "She didn't do it, and you know it. I reckon you know who did."

"Maybe it was you, then, if it wasn't her."

"He wasn't even on the ranch, not after he left that morning," Laura said. "You can't blame Ben for any of this. I got him into it, and he was only trying to help me. You must believe that!"

"I believe what I know . . . ," Marr began.

"But you're wrong about Ben!" Laura cried, her voice rising. "Do what you want with me! Keep the ranch, have me arrested for murder . . . but leave Ben out of it!"

"Don't waste your breath," Dunn said. "Marr knows what the truth is and that he's got to bury it with us . . . both of us. I won't have you beg him for my life."

"That there truth you're talkin' about," an older rider, apparently one of Isaac Pope's original hired hands, was speaking, "what you figure that is?"

Dunn saw Marr throw an angry glance at the cowboy. Before Marr could speak, Dunn said: "The truth is this . . . we didn't have anything to do with Pope's murder. And this *is* his daughter, Laura."

Marr quickly resumed control of the moment. He shrugged. "What else you expect him to say? Sure, he'll deny any charges we make. Wouldn't you if you were about to be strung up?"

Complete silence followed that. Marr waited a time, half turned in his saddle. "Harvey, you got those ropes?"

The tall rider came in nearer. He took the two lariats coiled loosely over his saddle horn, handed one to Sabine, the other to Frisco.

At sight of that, Laura uttered a small cry, turned to Ben and threw her arms about him. He held her for a moment, then moved her aside. When she was out of the way, he faced Marr. His hand hung close to the pistol at his hip.

Marr read his mind. "Don't try it," he warned softly. "There's half a dozen guns on you. And they won't shoot to kill, only to stop you from doing anything foolish. We're going to hang you, Dunn. You and your lady friend, too. That's the kind of justice you deserve and are going to get."

"Now, wait a minute here," the older cowpuncher, who had spoken up before, broke in. "I don't know about this hangin' a woman. . . ."

"What's the difference, Earl?" Marr demanded impatiently. "They were both in on it. They tried to euchre Pope out of his ranch by her claiming to be his daughter. When that didn't work, one of them killed him. And then to make it worse, they broke in and robbed the house while we were off burying the old man. If all that doesn't call for a hanging, I'd sure like to know what does!"

"He's a liar," Dunn stated calmly. "We had nothing to do with the murder. We were in the house during the funeral. We don't deny it. But we weren't robbing it. We were trying to find the proof we need to show that Laura is the daughter of Isaac Pope."

"Which you didn't find," Marr said.

Dunn nodded. "We didn't find it because you had already taken it."

Marr stirred. "No, because there wasn't any in the first place. That's just talk."

"Not quite," Dunn said coolly. "We found something that. . . ."

"You boys throw those ropes over that limb there," Marr broke in hastily. "Might as well hang them from the same tree. They run together, we'll let them swing together."

"Now, hold on, Jack!" Earl yelled, and rode forward from his position in the brush. "I'm for makin' anybody pay that killed Isaac, but I ain't so danged sure about this. And I ain't sure about hangin' a woman! I figure we better let the law have a hand in this."

Marr's voice was abruptly harsh. "Keep out of this, old man. If you're too chicken-hearted to do what's got to be done, then ride out. Go on back to the ranch and milk your cows."

Earl plucked at his stringy mustache. "Appears to me you're in an awful hurry to do this, Jack. You got some reason?"

"Reason? Here are two people who killed my pa in cold blood, and you ask me for a reason!"

The old cowboy moved his bony shoulders and spat. "Well, I don't reckon there's an argument against that, but I still don't cotton to stringin' up a woman. And they's some more of the boys here I 'spect feel the same way."

Harvey and another rider moved in behind Jack Marr. With Sabine and Frisco, they instantly became a tight, small group, threatening and ready for anything.

Marr said: "Earl, maybe you and the men you mentioned are tired of working for the Diamond X . . . and me. Maybe this would be a good time for you to pull stakes."

"Could be," the old cowpuncher replied agreeably. He studied the five men for a time. "You know, things ain't been right around the ranch since old Isaac got sick and you took over, Jack. It sure ain't no fittin' place for a man to

115

work cows no more. I'll just take your advice and give my notice now. . . ."

"I don't need any notice," Marr snapped. "Just be gone by the time I get back. If you got any wages coming, tell Harrison I said to pay you off." He pivoted about, threw his attention along the circle of riders. "Goes for all the rest of you, too. Now's the time to leave, if you've a mind to!"

Dunn, silent through the exchange and encouraged by the stubborn opposition on the part of Earl, saw another hope begin to dwindle away. He cast about for some means to hold the dissenters. He came up with a question.

"Any of you remember Pope had a wife?"

Earl, in the act of pulling away from the clearing, halted. He frowned, stared at Dunn. "Reckon I'm the oldest about the place and I don't recollect no such thing. 'Course, I come to work for Isaac about three years after he started up. Could have been before."

"Forget it," Marr cut in. "Move on, old man. I'm tired of your yammering. Pete, you and Bibo throw those ropes over that limb. Let's get on with this."

Dunn's attention swung to Marr. His face was stiff, grimly set. These were the last moments Laura and he would know. Of that he was certain. But he would make them count.

"If they do," he said to Marr, "you'll never live to see them finish the job. I promise you that, Marr."

"So? With a half a dozen slugs in you . . . what do you figure to do?"

"Still put one bullet in your heart," Dunn stated. "I'll have that much time."

From the edge of the clearing, Jay Greavey's voice said: "Hate to bust in on your little party, gents, but I claim first bite of this Dunn."

XVI

Startled, Marr swung about sharply. Sabine and Frisco again hesitated. Harvey, waiting for no cue, clawed at the pistol at his hip. A gunshot smashed through the hush. Harvey rocked on his saddle, sagged forward clutching at his shoulder.

Through a wisp of acrid powder smoke that drifted out into the clearing, Greavey said: "Seems there's always one joker that's got to prove how brave he is. Now, all of you just ease over there behind your boss so's I can keep an eye on you better."

The riders who had formed the tight semicircle around Laura Pope and Dunn immediately complied. They guided their mounts to positions back of and to the sides of Marr and the others.

"Fine, that's fine," Greavey drawled from his place beyond the screen of brush. "Don't know what this is all about, but I reckon it's got something to do with the killing of that rancher."

Marr said: "You're right. They murdered Isaac Pope . . . my pa. We were about to string them up for it."

"The girl, too?" Greavey asked, faint surprise in his voice. "Well, no truck of mine. But Dunn, there, is. He's a big man when it comes to killing, and, if you figure he killed this Pope, then I reckon he sure did. But I come first. He shot down my brother, and I've been a long time running him down to square that."

A glimmer of fresh hope rose within Ben Dunn, hope for Laura Pope, at least. He raised his arms, held his hands well

117

away from his sides to indicate he had no intention of going for his gun. Deliberately he pivoted about slowly, placed his back to Marr. He faced the point where Greavey, yet concealed, was standing.

"All right, Jay, you've caught up. I'm ready to have it out with you anytime you say. First, I'd like to make a bargain."

"A bargain?" Greavey said and laughed. "You ain't in such a good shape to bargain with me, Dunn."

"Not for myself, for the lady here. This whole thing is a trumped-up job. Marr is no real kin of Isaac Pope, but the girl here actually is his daughter. And neither one of us killed him."

"Wondered about you using a knife," Greavey commented. "Never knew you worked that way."

"Laura is the rightful owner of that ranch, but Marr and some of his private bunch are out to keep her from getting it."

"Some of them?"

"Yeah, the ones there in the middle. Rest of them ain't so sure. I'd like a chance to prove to them the girl is in the right."

Greavey did not immediately answer. Finally: "You trying to work some kind of a trick, Dunn?"

Ben shook his head. "No trick. Just don't want to see the girl get hurt. Once I've had my say, then it's you and me."

"Don't believe it!" Marr shouted. "He's got something up his sleeve!"

"How could I get away with anything?" Dunn demanded. "You're on one side of me, they're on the other. All I'm asking for is a chance to talk a few minutes and show a couple of tintypes in a book to prove what I say is the truth."

Greavey again considered at length. "What's in it for you?"

"Nothing for me," Ben said. "All for the lady. Don't like to stand by and see her get the worst of a deal, if I can help it."

"All right," Greavey said. "Reckon I owe you a favor. You could have put a bullet in me back there in the hills when that damned horse of mine fell. But I'm giving you warning. I don't trust you much. I'll be watching close. You make one wrong move, I'll break both your legs."

"You've got my word."

"Don't know if that's any good or not, and it don't make any difference one way or another. I'll just do my depending on my irons." He paused, continued: "Now, the rest of you saddle warmers set quiet until he's done. You listen to what he's got to say. In case you can't see me plain, I'm standing here with a Forty-Five in each hand. I can empty both of them into the pack of you before you could pull back a hammer. Just remember that and do your listening."

Dunn felt Laura's eyes on him, searching, wondering. He grinned down at her, exhibiting a confidence he was not too certain of himself.

"All right, bounty hunter," Greavey said, "it's your she-bang."

Dunn turned about, faced Marr and the silent group of Diamond X riders. "I don't figure to be much of a lawyer," he began, "and I've never had much practice talking out like this. But I reckon the truth is always easy to speak out. You heard me say Laura Pope is the daughter of Isaac and that we didn't have anything to do with killing him. Somebody else pulled that off to make it look bad for her. I don't think you'll have to go far to find out who's behind it. Figure a minute. If she *is* the heir of Pope, who would the Diamond X go to? Who would lose out?"

Dunn stopped, permitted the questions to have their effect. There was a stir among the riders.

"Reckon that would be Jack Marr," Earl said. "He'd lose out sure."

Ben nodded. "And right there's where I think you'll find the man who murdered Isaac Pope, or ordered it done."

There was a long minute of silence, then Jack Marr found his voice. "That's a damn' lie! He's trying to cover up. Pope never was married. . . ."

"I've got proof that he was," Dunn said calmly. "And he had a daughter." He turned, looked toward the invisible Greavey. "I'll have to get that book strapped to my saddle."

The gunman said: "Get it for him, lady."

Laura stepped quickly to the bay horse, untied the leather strings. She returned with the thick Bible, handed it to Dunn.

Ben wheeled back to Marr and the others. He noted Sabine and Frisco no longer held ropes. The coils now hung loosely over their saddles, leaving their hands free. He wondered if Greavey had also noticed the change.

He opened the book to its front page, held it up. "Here's the Pope family record. Shows the date he was married and gives the name of his wife. Then it shows a daughter was born. One of you step up here and take a look."

There was no response to the request. Finally Earl said: "Go on, Tom. Reckon you read letterin' better'n the rest of us. See what it says."

A young cowboy stirred himself, dismounted. He shouldered past Marr, halted a few steps from Dunn, glanced questioningly in Greavey's direction.

"Go right ahead," the gunman said. "Just keep your hands where I can see them."

The rider moved up to Ben who still held the book extended for him to see. He examined it for a few moments, stepped back.

"That's what it says," he announced, facing Earl and the rest. "Dates and all are there."

"Means nothing," Marr said. "Anybody could have written that in. The girl herself could have done it after they took that book from the house."

"How about these pictures, then?" Dunn said, and leafed to the back of the Bible where the tintype likenesses were framed in their ovals and squares. "You figure we did them, too?"

Tom studied the pages carefully. He scratched at his head, faced his friends. "He's sure right. These here pictures show old Isaac with a wife and kid, a baby girl. And there's writing saying who they are."

"But nothing to prove this girl is the same as the one in the pictures," Marr added, a note of triumph in his voice. "Seems to me all we know now is that Pope was married and had a daughter. No more than that."

"When Laura got here, she had that proof," Dunn said. "She showed it to Pope, and he accepted it, agreed that she was his daughter. There was a letter or two and a picture . . . one like these. But the night Pope was killed, it all disappeared. The picture, the letters, even the carpetbag she carried them in. . . ."

"Carpetbag?" Earl exclaimed. "That wouldn't be the one I saw you burnin' in the fireplace, would it, Bibo?"

There was a moment of stunned silence as the full meaning of the old cowboy's question drove home in the minds of the others.

"By God, Dunn's right!" somebody finally said. "This girl is old Isaac's daughter. And she wouldn't have done no killin'."

Ben felt a brief glow of satisfaction, of relief. Then he saw Sabine and Frisco suddenly hunch forward. He brushed Laura to one side with a sweep of his arm. His gun came up fast, bucked in his hand. He saw Marr level down on him even as he threw his first bullets into Sabine and Frisco.

Behind him he was vaguely aware of other guns firing, realized that Jay Greavey was having his say. He set himself for the smash of lead into his back. Miraculously there was none. Marr was falling from the saddle. Sabine was down. Frisco had buckled forward, arms dangling on either side of his horse's neck. Harvey had made no move to become a part of the skirmish. Like all the others, he sat with hands lifted. Understanding came then to Ben Dunn. Greavey had not fired on him, but had backed his play.

He drew himself up slowly. Keeping clearly in view of Greavey, he slid his revolver back into its holster. Laura, white and shaken, scrambled to her feet, rushed to him.

"Are you hurt?"

He said: "No, I'm fine." He swung his eyes to Marr, sprawled full length on the ground. "But I reckon that's all for Jack. And for Bibo and Pete."

"Oh, I'm so thankful!" she cried, throwing her arms about him. "All those guns! It was terrible . . . horrible!"

"It's over with now," he said, comforting her. He turned his attention to Earl and the remaining Diamond X men. "I take it you're satisfied the lady is Laura Pope?"

The old cowpuncher bobbed his head. "Ain't no doubt! Everything sure fits. And I allow it was Bibo that done the killin'. He looked after them kind of chores for Jack."

"Then take her home," Dunn said. "And have your boys load up those bodies and give them a burying."

He felt her stiffen against him. "I won't go," she declared, and clung to him. "I won't leave . . . I love you, Ben."

He held her close for a long minute. In that brief time the grim lines of his face softened, and then quickly hardened. "Take her," he said brusquely to Earl, who stood nearby. "And don't let her come back here."

He pulled away from the girl, wheeled toward the waiting Jay Greavey. He heard her sob and plead with the old cowpuncher to let her go.

"I can't! . . . I won't!" she cried.

He deafened himself to the sound of her voice and walked on. He halted near the center of the clearing. He did not move, nor did the gunman, until Laura and the others had ridden away. Only then did Jay Greavey show himself. He emerged from the brush, holstered his left side gun. The right was yet in his hand. He pulled to a stop a few paces in front of Dunn.

"You're a regular holy Joe!" he said, a sneer on his lips. "A real, genuine do-gooder. You changed some since the old days."

"Everything changes," Dunn said. "A thing you ought to realize."

"Tom's still dead," Greavey replied coldly. "Ain't nothing going to change that."

"And you think a shoot-out with me will?"

"Maybe not . . . except you'll be dead, same as him."

The small talk had begun to grind on Ben Dunn's nerves. He said: "Let's get on with it. No sense in standing here, doing all this jawing."

"You in a hurry to die?" the gunman asked. He was taking some sort of enjoyment from the delay. "You figure to go somewheres afterwards?"

"Maybe."

"Don't count on it," Greavey said. "I can take you, Dunn, any day in the week. If I didn't figure it so, I'd put a bullet in you now. But I want you to do some thinking these last few minutes while you're alive. Some thinking about that kid brother of mine."

"He was as bad as the worst of them. You know that."

"Got nothing to do with it. You started something you couldn't finish, and it's got to be settled by me."

Dunn shrugged. "You got that stuck in your mind. Like all your kind. Man sets himself up to believe a thing is one way. Was like that with me until a few years ago. Kept thinking about what had happened, what had gone before. Then it all changed. I found out it was easy to think about the present, even make a few plans for the future. Sure, I know a man can't get away from the past, but he doesn't have to keep on living it. And that's what you're doing. You're still living and fighting what used to be."

Greavey cocked his head in mock admiration. "You ought to have been one of them lawyers, instead of a bounty hunter!"

"You'd know what I say is true, if you'd let yourself think it over. What's done is done and us standing to in a gunfight won't prove anything now. Never has and never will. About all a man can do about the past is regret it . . . but there it ends."

Jay Greavey fondled the well-worn weapon in his hands. He hooked his right forefinger in the trigger guard, spun it expertly, then holstered it. "You wouldn't be trying to talk me out of killing you, would you, bounty man?"

Dunn said: "No. With a single track mind like you've got, you'd just go off somewhere, think about it for a spell, then come back. Your kind never learns anything until it's too late."

"Only time it's too late for a man is when he's dead."

"That's what I mean."

"You through talking out?"

"I'm ready when you are," Dunn replied.

"Gun of yours is about empty. You want to reload?"

"One bullet left in it. All I need."

Dunn saw the briefest flicker of uncertainty pass through Greavey's eyes and vanish. The gunman forced a laugh. "Mighty sure of yourself. You figure to get me with one bullet, that it?"

"Only takes one to kill a man."

Again Ben Dunn saw that moment of doubt in the gunman's gaze. He smiled faintly. "Thought you were in a hurry?"

Greavey shook his head. "Was just thinking about that woman. Sure going to be a shame, making her a widow before she even has a chance to marry up."

"Way the cards fall. She's a fine girl."

"Once knew a good woman . . . ," Greavey began, but Dunn's voice sliced through his words.

"Anytime, Jay."

The gunman's lips settled into a thin line. He began to back away, slowly, taking careful, precise half steps. Dunn remained motionless. He felt the man's eyes lock to his own, hold.

He saw a motion off to his right, beyond Jay Greavey. Abner Loveless walked into the clearing. He held an old, single barrel shotgun in his hands. It was pointed at Greavey.

"Hold up there, mister!" Loveless rasped. "What's this here all about, Ben?"

The gunman came to a halt. He did not remove his steady gaze from Dunn, merely suspended all movement.

"Raise up your hands!" Loveless ordered, walking in a step nearer.

It was a way out, an easy way. That thought flashed through Ben Dunn's mind as he saw Greavey slowly lift his arms. He didn't know if he could match the gunman's speed with a revolver or not; there was a good chance he could fail, that he would die in the shoot-out. A man can get rusty, go stale. But to call it off solved nothing. It was not the answer, for Greavey would come again. He would have his try.

He said: "Forget it, Abner. Stay out of this."

The shotgun in Loveless's hand lowered. "That what you want?"

"It's what I want."

Dunn watched Greavey. The gunman's arms dropped slowly to his sides. His face was expressionless, only that dead, empty stare. He had found a distance and position to his liking and no longer backed away. Ben shut out all else from his consciousness, concentrating on Greavey alone. He tried to recall what he knew of the man, of his style. Was he the sort who lunged to one side when he fired? Or did he dip forward, go down low as so many fast guns were inclined to do? He could not remember. It had been so long ago.

Suddenly Greavey was in action. His right hand was an upsweeping blur. His body twisted slightly left. Dunn threw himself forward. His own weapon smashed out its sound, even before he completed the move.

He felt Greavey's bullet drive into his shoulder and weathered the spasm of pain as it shattered bone. He saw Greavey spin, complete a full turn. He realized his slug had caught the gunman as he twisted. Greavey went to his knees, struggled to rise. His mouth was open, his features distorted. He fought to lift the gun in his hand and level it. Abruptly he was without strength. He fell heavily, going full length.

Numbed by the bullet, Dunn stood motionless while Abner Loveless crossed the clearing, halted beside the gunman. He kicked Greavey's revolver off into the brush, peered down into the man's chalk-white face.

"He's dead," Loveless said, straightening up. "You got him almost dead center. What was this here ruckus all about? Don't recollect ever seein' him around before."

"An old score," Ben said, "finally settled." His head was beginning to spin a little. He walked slowly to the well, leaned against the wooden housing.

"You and Hopeful all right?" he asked. "Heard you'd been burned out."

"We're all right," Loveless said. "Say, looks like you're hit right good." He swung around, faced the brush. "Hopeful, come over h'yar! Ben's gone and got hisself shot. Needs some doctorin'."

Abner poured a dipper of water, held it to Dunn's lips. "You need somethin' stronger'n this, but I reckon it'll have to do."

Hopeful Loveless came bustling into the clearing. She had apparently been waiting in the brush until Abner was sure of what was taking place. She began at once to tend Dunn's wound, making little clucking noises as she worked.

Abner glanced about the yard. "I'd say old Bibo and Pete and that other feller paid you a little visit, too," he remarked. "Say, where's the little gal?"

"Riding for the Pope place," Dunn said. He related the previous encounter that had ended with the death of Marr and his two men. "Everything is squared for her now. Guess Diamond X has got a new boss."

Abner Loveless was looking beyond him, to the edge of the clearing. "Maybe so, but she sure ain't headed for her ranch."

Dunn was suddenly aware of Laura's presence at his side. He turned to face her.

"I had to come," she said. "When I heard those gunshots, I had to come back. Oh, Ben, are you hurt badly?"

"Bullet in the shoulder, that's all."

"Be all right, soon as we get him to some doctoring," Hopeful said, completing the bandage.

"Then it's all over and done with," Laura said in a thankful voice.

Dunn glanced at Greavey. "He's only one. Likely there will be more."

"We won't worry about them," she said. "And if they come, we'll face them together. Right now we've got to get you to our ranch and take care of your arm."

"Where?" he wondered.

She smiled at him. "To our ranch," she repeated. "And we've got plenty of room for Abner and Hopeful if they want to come along."

The old cowboy grinned broadly. "I reckon you just hired yourself a couple of new hands, ma'am," he said. "Let's get started for home!"

Valley of the Wandering River

1

He rode in from the north, a lean, gray-eyed man with a sun- and wind-burned face, sitting high-shouldered on a red sorrel gelding. When he passed through the narrow gash in the rock-walled crest of the San Geronimos and looked down into Wandering River Valley, a sigh slipped from his lips, and for a brief time the flint-like quality in his glance softened. A sort of ease came over him, and, leaning forward, he rested a forearm on the horn of his scarred, double-rigged saddle and took in the broad, lush panorama spread before him.

Once they'd called it Chant's Valley, after his pa, who had been the first to settle along Wandering River. But that was a day long ago—twenty-five, maybe thirty years past. When others began to move in, a new name caught on— Wandering River Valley—and thus it became known.

Dave Chant guessed it was all right. The river had been there at the start. It was only natural that the surrounding country take its name from that source and not from the man who pioneered the area—a man not held in great esteem by those who came to live nearby and know him. But it would have been a fine tribute to the old man just the same.

He shifted slightly and raised his gaze from the meandering silver thread of the river, with its edging of bright green cottonwoods, to the grayer hued sage to the east. That twist of smoke would be Chamisa—a dozen or so buildings assembled shoulder to shoulder along a solitary, dusty main street. Chamisa . . . he could recall how he and

Cliff, his half-brother, had used to run along the board side-walks, staring into each of the store windows at the assortment of merchandise displayed therein. They'd made a game of it while their parents shopped in Toteman's General Store. Each alternately claimed a window, and all that was visible behind the dust-covered glass became that one's private property.

His favored stop had always been Hansen's Gun Shop, where he would stand for uncounted minutes staring at the sleek weapons—the long-barreled pistols, the snub-nosed Derringers that only gamblers carried, the small, pearl-handled hide-out guns, the rifles, some with intricately engraved parts and carved stocks. Cliff, five years his junior, had been taken more by what he saw in Abousleman's Saddle and Harness Store and in Toteman's, where he could find a little of everything. Toteman's was fine, Dave had been forced to admit on occasion, particularly the smells, but nothing could displace the fascination the assortment of weapons instilled within him each time he looked in Hansen's.

A long time ago, Dave thought. A score of years, at least, during which many things had changed. He and Cliff had grown up, hardened. A feeling had come between them, one bordering upon hatred, engendered no doubt by the death of their mother, further fostered by the bitterness that claimed Jared Chant and his gradual turning to his younger son to the exclusion of Dave.

The favoritism cut deeply at first, but Dave learned to live with it, perhaps even understood it a little, to the point where often he shouldered the blame for Cliff's misdeeds rather than see his father's disappointment. But that, too, like the child's games they'd played grew old, and the day came when Dave struck out on his own, leaving parent,

132

brother, home, and all the memories, good and bad, behind. It hadn't been hard to do; Jared Chant had made no bones about which son stood taller in his mind.

Perhaps it had come to pass of his own making. While Cliff was apparently a rancher at heart, professing interest in cattle and the problems that went with the raising of beef, Dave was more of the born-free nature with a love for riding and an intense interest in becoming adept with the pistol he'd saved his pennies and nickels for. Jared Chant had disapproved of that violently, although Dave was sixteen at the time. To keep peace in the house, he had hidden the weapon from his father's sight, done his practicing on the range well beyond gunshot hearing of the ranch.

Cliff would be running the Box C by now, he guessed. His pa would be somewhere in his sixties, if he reckoned correctly, and no longer very active where ranch chores were concerned. But he could be wrong. Jared Chant had been a whang leather tough man; he could still be ramrodding things just as he had in the old days, and Cliff, just as in the past, would be taking orders, scurrying about doing Pa's bidding, living in the shadow of his parent.

There was nothing wrong with that, Dave supposed, if that was what Cliff wanted—and he guessed he'd even been thinking a bit along those lines himself for the last year or two. There was something to be said for a man having his own place, digging in, building something he could call his own. Cliff would have that day—when Jared Chant was gone. But Dave . . . well, he'd seen the country border to border; he'd made a name for himself, earned the respect of men from whom respect was hard to come by, and. . . . And? At least he'd been free—free and alive so long as he kept his gun thonged to his thigh and never relaxed his vigilance day or night. He'd earned that, too, but there was a hell of a price tag on it, and lately he was beginning to tire, only slightly, perhaps, but tire nevertheless of the never-ending tension.

Maybe it would be good to stop, to hang up his gun, and think about a different way of life. Possibly there was room for him on the Box C. It was a big spread, largest in the valley, and he'd heard beef prices were high in the market places—eighteen dollars a head, he'd been told. He could make peace with his father, and, as far as Cliff was concerned, they'd get along. Cliff could run the ranch, as he likely was doing; he'd be there to help, take orders—and handle any trouble when and if it arose.

Dave Chant shifted again on the sorrel, now fidgeting restlessly, and swung his gaze to the south. The Box C lay there, over beyond a grove of trees. Probably those cattle he could see ranging back up the long slope to Dead Horse Mesa were Box C stock. The house and other structures he could not see; Jared Chant had built them in a slight hollow not far from a towering bluff that sheltered them from the storms coming out of the north in winter.

There'd been a sign hanging from chains over the gate that led into the yard. **BOX C RANCH. J. CHANT & SONS** it read. Dave wondered if the sign was still there, if it had been changed. Seven years was a long time to be away—and not once during his absence had he written a single line or forwarded word of his well-being. For all Jared and Cliff Chant knew, he was dead. If that sign had been altered, he could blame no one but himself.

The urge to settle all such questions and doubts possessed him, and, touching the sorrel lightly with his spurs, he started down the long slope for the floor of the valley. It would take a good two hours to reach the Box C—two hours in which to iron out his thoughts, figure what he wanted to say when he faced his father. He'd brought a peace offering. Many times he'd heard Jared Chant mention a desire for a barometer—a shipmaster's glass, he'd termed it. No such instrument had been available in that part of the country, not even in the larger towns of Dalhart or Dodge City.

Dave guessed that his seeing such an instrument one day in a seacoast shop in Oregon had been partly responsible for the idea of going home. He'd been up there doing a job for a Wyoming cattleman, and the thought had come to him. He'd bought the glass, had it carefully packed, and then stowed it away in his saddlebags. When he'd finished the job—locating and returning to the Wyoming rancher the man who'd murdered the rancher's brother—he had headed south.

Maybe the bit of brass would break the ice with Jared, make it easier to talk. Dave hoped so, but he reckoned he could not blame his father too much if he was still unwelcome. If such proved to be the case, he'd ride on until he reached El Paso, he decided, looking out over the slopes vivid with yellow and purple June flowers. It had been quite a spell since he'd visited the border city, and, although it would be necessary for him to keep clear of the law while there, he supposed he could manage it. That old murder charge would be cleared up someday—leastwise, he hoped so. But things like that took time, it seemed.

He reached the grove of cottonwoods and paused in the shade to rest the sorrel. The sun was hot—unusually so for June. And then he remembered that the temperature in the valley had always been high, once the winter months were gone. Pocketed between the San Geronimos to the east and north, Dead Horse Mesa on the west, and a searing desert to the south, it was a land that accumulated and retained heat. Why, there had been some winters when, on Christmas day he and Cliff had played in the yard wearing no more than cotton shirts and overalls.

Dave Chant shrugged off the thoughts of what had been, weary of them. This was now—a lifetime later—and there was no sense in mulling over the old days. Impatient, he swung to the saddle and rowelled the big horse into a fast lope. The sooner he reached the ranch and faced up to Jared Chant, the quicker he'd know where he stood—and what his future would be.

He angled through the grove, broke out onto a wide flat, and struck a faint trail that bore west. To his right now was the sheltering bluff, and then somewhat later he saw the cluster of buildings that made up the Box C—unchanged through the years, it appeared. But there was change at the gate. No sign at all hung from the dangling chains that had squeaked so dryly when the wind blew—no sign at all. That struck Dave Chant as strange. His father had been proud of that oak and pine pennant which so rigidly proclaimed his ownership. He might alter its lettering, but he'd never remove it.

He rode on, passed beneath the high, naked beam, slanted toward the low-roofed, rambling ranch house, eyes sweeping back and forth as they gathered in the old familiar places and evoked long forgotten scenes. Abruptly a rifle shot cracked through the warm hush. The sorrel reared as dust spurted between his forelegs.

"Close enough!" a voice barked from the brush at the corner of the house.

II

Cool, Dave Chant quieted the sorrel and held his eyes on the squat, thick-shouldered man moving into the yard. The metallic *click* of the rifle's action was loud as a fresh cartridge was levered into the chamber. Chant searched the rider's dark face closely and found no recognition. This dispelled the thought first to reach his mind—that he had encountered an old enemy from some distant time and trail. This was a stranger, not even someone he could recall from the days of his boyhood.

"Your welcome's a mite unfriendly," he drawled.

The squat cowpuncher pulled up short. "And it's going to get a hell of a lot unfriendlier if you don't cut that horse around and get out of here."

Dave continued to study the man, the house and other buildings beyond his threatening shape. Two riders were watching from near the barn. The cook had come from a side door of the house and was leaning against the wall, wiping his hands on a dirty, ragged apron.

"Don't recollect ever seeing you around here before."

"Makes us even," the cowpuncher said. "Ain't never seen you, either. Now you turn that horse around and. . . ."

"Looking for Jared Chant, owner of the place. He around?"

"Sure ain't."

The tone of the reply sent a stream of surprise through Dave, and then a dull suspicion began to grow within him. "Know where I can find him?"

"Heaven or hell . . . all depending."

Chant stiffened. "That mean he's dead?"

"Reckon it does, mister. Now, I ain't. . . ."

"How about his son Cliff? Any idea where I can find him?"

"I sure as hell don't, and, what's more, I'm done answering your questions. If you. . . ."

"Hate putting you to so much bother," Dave said mildly, "but the only way a man can get answers is to ask questions. Mind telling me who owns this ranch now?"

"I don't mind, but I just ain't," the cowpuncher snapped.

"Is it a secret or something?"

"Hell, no, it ain't no secret! I plain figure it ain't none of your business. And, besides, I got something else to do besides standing here jabbering with you."

"You reckon one of those boys back there by the barn'll know where I can find Cliff Chant? Or maybe, if I was to ask the cook . . . ?"

"You ain't doing nothing but getting off this here ranch," the cowpuncher said flatly. "Boss don't like drifters poking around, cluttering up the place. I got orders to shoot . . . keep the likes of you off."

"Can't see no harm just riding up to the door, asking a question. What's he scared of?"

"What's who scared of?"

Chant eased slightly on the sorrel, edging the big horse a step to the left. The corner of the house now shut off the view of the cook. Frowning angrily, the squat man followed.

"That boss you're talking about," Dave said.

"He ain't scared of nothing . . . not him! Just don't want every saddle tramp from hell to hallelujah sashaying across his property."

"Seems a mighty inhospitable critter," Chant murmured, raising his glance. The two men near the barn had disappeared. "Wish I knew his name."

The stocky rider, face flushed, lifted his rifle and crowded up close. "I'm telling you for the last time. . . ."

Dave Chant was off the saddle in a single move. With his left hand he wrenched the weapon from the cowpuncher's hand, with the right he delivered a stinging slap to his face.

"Hey! You. . . ."

Wheeling, Chant threw the rifle far out into the blue gray-sage bordering the yard, and then spun as the man stooped to pick up a short length of wood lying nearby. Chant, swinging his right again, this time knotted into a rock-hard fist, caught the rider on the side of the head, driving him to his knees.

Temper riding him, he surged in, caught the cowpuncher by the collar, flung him backward into the dust. Then, leaning over, he glared into the rider's startled face.

"I'm through horsing around with you," he snarled. "I'm asking the same questions again, and you'd better have the answers if you ever aim to get up!"

The squat man's features twisted angrily. An oath exploded from his lips, and he made a sudden effort to rise. Just as suddenly he relaxed, settled back as the muzzle of Chant's pistol was abruptly pressing against his head. Eyes open wide, he stared. The weapon had appeared so swiftly, so smoothly, that he had failed even to see the motion of Chant's arm.

"Told you all I know," he mumbled.

"You real sure you don't know where Cliff Chant is?"

"Honest, I don't. Only been working here a month or so.

Never did hear nobody mention it."

"What about Jared Chant? That the truth about him being dead?"

"Reckon it is . . . for a fact."

"How'd it happen?"

"Don't rightly know. Was before I came along. Expect he just up and died. He . . . he some sort of special friend of yourn?"

Dave stepped back, holstered his pistol. "I guess you'd say special," he replied, glancing toward the barn.

"Ain't no use you going back there, talking to them boys, either," the cowpuncher said. "Hired on about same time as me. . . . It all right if I get up?"

Chant nodded. Best thing would be to ride into Chamisa. He could find out what the score was from Toteman or Hansen or one of the other merchants. They'd likely know where Cliff was, too. There was nothing to be learned here; either the men didn't know, or they were afraid to talk.

He studied the cowpuncher, dusting off his clothing with his hat. "Who'd you say owned this place now?"

The man paused, glanced up slyly. "Didn't say. Howsomever, my boss is Pete Hawley. Ramrods the outfit. You see him, you ask him who the owner is."

Dave nodded absently. Abruptly he whirled, drove his fist again into the cowpuncher's jaw. The man staggered to one side, came up against the hitch rack, caught himself, and hung there. Dazed, astonishment blanking his features, he stared at Chant, now swinging back onto the saddle.

"Now, why'd you do that? I. . . ."

"Giving you a little lesson in manners," Chant said dryly. "Next time somebody comes riding up asking for in-

140

formation, maybe you'll remember to give him a civil answer or two."

Nodding pleasantly, he wheeled the sorrel about and moved toward the gate.

III

It wasn't the Chamisa he'd known, turned his back upon seven years ago. A dozen new structures lined the street—a new feed store, another barbershop, a restaurant, several saloons. Where Hansen's had stood, there was a men's clothing store that specialized in perfect fit boots, so the sign declared. Abousleman's place was boarded up. Toteman's no longer existed—the building that had once housed it was now quarters for a gambling and dance hall.

There was a stage depot, next door to the Prairie Hotel, and that sent a ripple of surprise through Dave Chant. Chamisa was finally on the coach route. Merchants had always hoped for it, and now it was reality. Something else was new—at the far end of the street a large two-story building had been erected. Huge black letters on its false front and down the side designated it as **BARR'S EMPORIUM**. In smaller printing slightly below was added: **Everything for Everybody**.

Dave considered that for a time, and then brushed his hat to the back of his head. Chamisa looked like a new town—a real boomer. Everyone seemed to have painted and cleaned up, given all things possible a going over. Something must have happened to jar the residents to such activity, and all the old names were gone.

Dave frowned, thinking of that truth, and put the sorrel into motion down the center of the street at a slow walk. A dozen or so persons were about, strolling along the boardwalk. A man standing in front of a livery stable appeared familiar, but he did not speak, and Chant could find no name to fit him, thus he couldn't be sure. The bank was still on the corner. The words **AARON FABER, PRESIDENT** on the door struck a chord, but he'd never known Faber. He only recalled the name vaguely.

The marshal's office, directly opposite and bearing a new coat of white paint, was in the same location. The lawman's name was Frazier, Dave thought, but he was not certain. . . . Just as well. No good had ever come to him from a lawman. Best he seek information elsewhere.

Kinsvater's Saloon. Seeing that familiar name sent a sigh of relief through him and offered the answer to his problem. The narrow-fronted structure was now a flaming red, and a new porch floor had been installed along with fancy, scrolled swinging doors—but it was still Kinsvater's. It was like encountering an old friend in a land filled with strangers.

He leaned forward, quickening the sorrel's pace, and then, as he drew abreast of the marshal's office, he settled back slowly. The lawman had appeared abruptly and was moving into the street to intercept him.

Another stranger. Frazier had been a big, round-bellied man with pleasant, easy-going features. Here was a thin, hawk-faced individual with a grim, set jaw, sharp, suspicion-filled black eyes, and graying hair worn almost to the shoulders in the style of Bill Hickok.

"Haul in, Chant," the marshal ordered gruffly.

Dave groaned silently. It would be his luck to meet a badge that knew him. Shrugging, he cut the sorrel toward the hitch rail, pulled to a stop, and waited.

"Climb down."

Chant, his movements deliberate, swung down from the saddle. Face set, he looped the leathers around the crossbar and turned to the lawman.

"What's this about?"

"Inside," the marshal said, ducking his head toward the open door to his office. "We're having a little talk."

Dave leaned against the rack. "What you've got to say to me can be said right here."

"Reckon it can, but I don't aim to draw no attention. Inside."

Chant shrugged, stepped up onto the walk, crossed, and entered the combination office and jail. Halting in the center of the room, he turned to the lawman.

"Seems you know me. I don't know you."

"You wouldn't . . . all things considered," the marshal replied, crossing to his desk and sitting on a corner. "The name's Sloan. Harry Sloan."

"Man wearing the badge when I was last here was named Frazier."

"Dead five years. Outlaws holding up the bank got him. Brings me to you. What're you here for?"

"Not to rob the bank," Dave said, anger beginning to stir him. "Any law says a man can't visit his hometown?"

"Ordinarily, no. But a man like you. . . ."

"What happened to my pa?" Chant cut in abruptly. "Understand he's dead."

Sloan sighed deeply, pulled away from the desk, and settled heavily in his chair. His mouth sagged wearily. "So that's what brought you. Might've known."

Dave Chant's senses drew keenly alert. The lawman's action had meaning of some sort. Arms folded, he stared at Sloan's craggy features, rode out a long minute.

"Giving you to understand right now, Chant. I'll stand for no trouble around here. Makes no difference who you are. Reputation don't scare me one whit."

"No reason it should. Far as trouble's concerned, it's not up to me."

"Done all I could to run down your pa's killer. Just wasn't enough to go on."

Killer! Jared Chant had been murdered! Choosing his words carefully to mask his own lack of information, Dave said: "Not clear to me when it happened. How long ago?"

"Two months, more or less."

Chant stirred irritably. It had taken him seven years to return—and he'd made it two months too late.

"No point in your blowing in, stirring up things," Sloan said, his voice again edged.

"Is there something that can be stirred up?"

Sloan frowned. "Nope . . . not a damned thing. Your pa was dry-gulched for the money he was carrying. Likely was some drifter who done it. Ends right there, and I'll not have you coming around trying to make more'n that out of it. You hear me, Chant?"

"Hadn't given much thought. . . ."

"Well, give this some thought," the lawman said coldly. "Can't stop you from riding through, but I can sure as hell keep you from hanging around."

"Maybe. I'm not wanted in this town, Marshal. You know that."

"Sure I know it, but I reckon I can walk right over to the telegraph office, send out a couple, three telegrams, and find somebody who does. And mister, that's what I'll do if you give me cause."

"You just do that," Chant snapped, equally warm. "But something about this deal smells bad to me. I've got a mind to find out what it is."

Harry Sloan came to his feet slowly. Jaw thrust forward, he glared at Chant. "Meaning you aim to hang around?"

Dave nodded. "Until I know what's been going on."

"I've told you."

145

"Then what's making you so damned anxious for me to keep moving?"

"One thing . . . we've got a good, clean town here. Growing every day. New people are moving in right along. Got some Eastern money interested in us, helping us make something of the place. And. . . ."

"And a man like me's not welcome."

"Exactly. We've no place for gunslingers. Nothing but bad news wherever you and your kind are. Gives any place a bad name, scares newcomers away. We don't want your kind around, and it's my job to see that. . . ."

"You're getting all lathered up over nothing, Marshal. I'll give you and your town no trouble."

Sloan shook his head. "Hard to believe that. Trouble just naturally trails along with your kind." He paused, pointed to the weapon thonged to Chant's leg. "You willing to leave that with me . . . guarantee. . . ."

"You know better than to ask that, Sloan," Dave cut in. "Everybody else around here is packing iron. I'd be a fool not to wear mine."

"Wear it, then!" the lawman said, his voice rising angrily. "But, by God, you keep it hooded! Understand?"

It was an old Army expression that had reference to the flap on a holster, but Chant got the meaning.

"Long as nobody gives me cause, you've got my word."

"Your word," Sloan echoed in a mocking tone.

"Something I've not broken to any man, Marshal, whether you believe it or not," Chant said stiffly. "You had your say?"

"I have. Where you figure to put up?"

"The Prairie," Dave said, and, spinning on a heel, returned to the street.

IV

Chant halted beside the sorrel, hand on the reins. Anger was flowing through him steadily—anger and bitter frustration that stemmed from his own helplessness. Because he was Dave Chant, he was denied the simple facts concerning the death of his father, because he was Dave Chant, he was forbidden, under penalty of arrest, the opportunity to look into the matter, learn what had taken place. The hell with it! The hell with Marshal Harry Sloan and the town he was so anxious to see boom! He'd find out the score one way or another.

He'd find out about Cliff, too. In his flush of anger he'd neglected to ask the lawman about his brother. Just as well. Likely he would have got the same, careful runaround. Why all the secrecy, the closed-mouth treatment where Jared Chant's death was concerned? The rider at the Box C claimed to know nothing about it—or the whereabouts of Cliff. If he had told the truth, then it would appear to be a forbidden subject on the ranch. If he had lied, it was also proof that the topic was to be avoided.

Insofar as Harry Sloan was concerned, the marshal had divulged only the barest facts—if facts they were. No details, no information of note that carried meaning and that a son would ordinarily be entitled to when inquiring about the death of a parent. Was the lawman covering up? Was he hiding something, using the story of the town's hoped-for growth as a reason to keep Dave moving on, unwilling to let him turn up a few stones for fear he would discover something that would upset somebody's coal wagon?

Chant swung half around, thoughtfully considered the marshal's office. He could see Sloan through the window, sitting at his desk. The lawman glanced up, returned his gaze with steady intentness. It would be useless to press him for more information, Dave realized. He'd get nowhere, and it would serve only to antagonize the old lawman further.

He turned away, jerked the sorrel's reins free, and swung onto the saddle. Go on to Kinsvater's, as he had planned to do in the first place. Surely he'd be able to find out a few details there.

There were only half a dozen or so patrons in the saloon when he entered. An aged and crippled swamper was sweeping up last night's litter near the doorway—and the man behind the bar was not Kinsvater. Dave touched the customers with an impersonal glance as he crossed the room, saw no one he knew, and halted at the long, polished counter.

"Whiskey," he said, leaning on his elbows. As the round-faced bartender reached for a bottle and glass, he added: "Kinsvater around?"

"Santa Fé," the man replied, sliding the drink to him. "Two bits."

Chant laid a dollar on the counter. "He coming back today?"

"Ain't much chance of it. Visiting his kin. Don't look for him for a couple more weeks. Something I can maybe do for you?"

"I'm Dave Chant. Trying to locate my brother. Was hoping Kinsvater could tell me where he'd gone."

The hush that dropped over the saloon was immediate. Chant saw quick withdrawal fill the barkeep's eyes and a stillness came over his features.

"Can you tell me?"

The man shrugged. "Sure can't."

Dave turned about, hooked his elbows on the edge of the counter, and glanced over the room. "Seems my pa's been murdered, too. Like to hear a few details on that. Anybody here willing to fill me in?"

The swamper ceased his sweeping, regarding Chant thoughtfully. The men at the tables and ranged along the bar made no sound. After a long minute Chant stirred impatiently.

"Damned funny thing," he said, scorn tingeing his words. "One man gets murdered, another disappears, and nobody knows anything. What's going on around here?"

A heavy-set man at the end of the bar rubbed nervously at his chin. "Might try asking the marshal. He ought to. . . ."

"Talked to him. Didn't do much good."

"Then I reckon there ain't much to know," the bartender said dryly.

Chant, sudden anger gusting through him, whirled swiftly. His arm shot out. His fingers caught the barkeep's shirt front, jerking him hard against the counter. Glasses rattled, and a bottle toppled, rolled, and fell to the floor with a crash.

"There's plenty to know . . . and I aim to find out what it is!" Dave snarled, holding the man pinned to the counter.

The barkeep swallowed convulsively. "Ain't nothing I can tell you, mister. Maybe Kinsvater . . . when he gets back. . . ."

"Can't wait that long," Chant said, shoving the man away, and again looking over the room.

The heavy-set man was again clawing at his chin. "Ain't sure I know who you're asking about."

"You know," Chant replied harshly. "Jared Chant. He was the first man to settle this country. Used to call it after him . . . Chant's Valley. Cliff's his son. They've been running the Box C ranch all these years . . . and you don't think you're ever heard of them?"

"Well, I'm a sort of a Johnny-Come-Lately. . . ."

Chant's tone was thick with disgust. "You've heard of them, all right." He glanced around the saloon. "It's been seven years since I was in this town. Plenty of changes, for sure. Mostly, however, change seems to be in the kind of men living here nowadays."

Wheeling, he stalked toward the door. The old swamper, having worked his way onto the porch, was picking up his sweepings, dumping them into a bucket. He did not pause as Dave moved through the batwings.

"Don't let on I'm talking to you, Mister Chant," he murmured. "Reckon you don't recollect me."

"You look familiar . . . just can't remember your name," Chant said, gazing off into the street. The Emporium seemed to have a corner on the town's business. A half a dozen rigs were drawn up before the building.

"I'm Heber. Used to hostle down at Billy Magee's stable when you was just a button."

"Sure. Comes to me now. Got that arm of yours all bunged up by a wild stallion."

"Yes. . . . When Billy quit business, I took this here job. Now, I'm going to be toting this bucket around back to empty it. You give me a minute or two, then follow. I'll be standing in the shed."

Dave moved to the edge of the porch, continued to stare off into the distance. Heber shoveled up the last of the trash, leaned his broom against the front of the building, and, taking the bail of his bucket, ambled off toward the rear of the structure.

Chant crossed leisurely to the sorrel, paused to tighten the cinch and make other slight adjustments. Finally he stepped into the leather. Settling himself, he looked again to the Emporium for several moments, and then pulled away from the rail.

Cutting right, he walked the red horse down the vacant lot that separated Kinsvater's from the building standing to the south, immediately dropping from view of anyone in the street. Spotting the shed the old swamper had mentioned, he angled toward it and halted at not too close a distance.

"Heber?"

"Right here, Mister Chant. You see anybody watchin'?"

Dave glanced about casually. "Nobody, far as I can tell. There something you want to say?"

"A little . . . not much. But your pa was good to me. Figure I owe it to him to tell what I know."

"Any idea who bushwhacked him?"

"Nope. Sure can't help you none there. Whoever it was got him from the back, then robbed him."

"How about Cliff? What happened to him?"

"Got hisself shot up real bad. You'll find him out at the Gannon place. Him and the Gannon gal was fixing to marry up . . . then all this happened."

Dave Chant held his eyes straight ahead. "What's going on around here, Heber? Everybody acts like he's walking on eggs, afraid to open his mouth."

"Things has really changed since that Andrew Barr come in, spending all kinds of money, putting his fancy store. . . ."

"The Emporium?"

"Yeah, that's it. He's making a lot of what he calls investments, too. And then there's that gun-hawk of his . . .

Wooton. Reckon he's the main reason nobody ever does any talking. Nobody wants to get crossways with him."

"But if Pa was bushwhacked by some outlaw, and Cliff's out at Gannon's, what's wrong with talking about it?"

"Nothing, far as I can see, but folks don't. Could be they was warned . . . and nobody wants to get in bad with Barr and Wooton. It's kind of like you said inside . . . the looks of the town ain't the only thing that's changed."

Chant shifted lazily on the saddle, fished a coin from his pocket. "Expect I'd better ride out, see Cliff. Maybe he can tell me a few things."

"Expect he'll be the only one. You tell him for me I'm hoping he's coming along all right."

"I'll do it," Dave said, dropping the coin. "When you come out, there's a gold eagle on the ground here."

"You don't have to do that. Your pa. . . ."

"This is from me, not my pa. I'm obliged to you, Heber."

"You're mighty welcome, son. Good luck."

V

Chant rode slowly across the vacant lot. When he came to the alley that ran behind the buildings, he swung south, moving to the rear of the first structure. A store of some kind, he noted, seeing the stack of empty packing crates arranged neatly at the end of a wagon bed high loading platform.

Motion at the door drew his attention. He watched a man wearing black satin sleeve guards step into the doorway, eye him speculatively, and withdraw. Another new merchant, Dave thought, and wondered if there were any of the old bunch other than Kinsvater still doing business in Chamisa.

Tom Gannon and his family were still in the valley. There was comfort in that knowledge. The two families—the Gannons and the Chants—had been neighbors for many years. Their property lines adjoined, and once there had been talk of combining the two into a huge spread that would dominate the valley. Nothing had come of it. Jared Chant's independent nature refused to permit his going into a partnership with anyone.

Reaching the edge of the settlement, Dave Chant cut the sorrel off onto the road pointing due west, following the deep ruts with their grassy shoulders until he reached the first of the low bluffs marking the east bank of Wandering River. There he abandoned the road, and, ignoring the plank bridge that spanned the stream at its narrowest point, he rode down to the water and followed along its course for a full mile. It was an old trail, one that would save him a good half hour's ride in reaching Gannon's Triple X.

It had been a good spring, Chant noticed, as the sorrel moved on steadily. Rains had apparently been plentiful, and bright patches of purple, yellow, and red wildflowers splashed the slopes and flats all around him. Even the sage was rich blue and thick, and in the low places crown-beard already stood waist-high with buds that promised blossoms as large as their sunflower kinsmen.

The huge cottonwood that marked the spot where he used to ford the river had blown down. It now lay partially submerged in the swift, quiet water, victim no doubt of some violent storm. But oddly it still lived. A wealth of bright green leaves shimmered, crown-like, in the upper branches, and clusters of the small, cotton-filled grapes locally called *tatones* could be seen throughout the tangle of limbs.

The sorrel splashed through the knee-deep stream, clambered up onto the opposing bank, and halted as Chant drew him in, wanting to have a look at the river winding off between the trees and salt cedars below. At that moment Dave heard the dull thud of an approaching horse moving up the trail behind him. Frowning, he twisted on the saddle to look. It was not a course customarily followed—he doubted if anyone other than Cliff ever used the route. But someone was on it now.

The inner caution of the man sent up its warning flags, and at once Chant spurred around the fallen cottonwood, hurried toward a thick stand of brush a dozen yards farther down the edge of the river. Pulling well into the screen, he halted and turned to watch. It could be nothing more than a cowpuncher hunting strays—and it could be someone trailing him.

Moments later the rider broke into view. Astride a blaze-faced bay, he came to the cottonwood and pulled to a stop on the opposite side of the stream. Chant gave him close scrutiny and sighed. Another stranger.

He was a big man, both tall and heavily built. About thirty, Dave guessed, dark and with a long scar running eyebrow to jawbone, a thick nose, and a hard set to his mouth. He wore a pistol low on his right leg, and a rifle was cradled in his arms.

For a time the stranger remained quiet, moving only his head as he looked up and down the river's banks. Finally he swung from the saddle and, climbing out onto the horizontal trunk of the cottonwood, resumed his careful search of the surrounding country.

No doubt remained in Dave Chant's mind at this point—the scar-faced man had been tracking him, whether from curiosity or for purpose he could not be sure. He had a momentary urge to ride out of the brush, confront the man, and determine which. Then, recalling Marshal Harry Sloan's warning and considering the way of things in the valley, he had second thoughts. He must be content with only the knowledge that he had been followed. Best to find out the reason behind it before he made any move. It could have definite bearing on the problem that he'd found facing him in Wandering River Valley.

Abruptly the rider turned, picked his way back along the tree trunk, dropped to firm ground. There he stood for a space of time studying the gravelly edge of the water and then, shrugging, returned to his horse. Mounting, he wheeled and retraced his course toward town.

Dave gave him a full quarter hour before moving out of the brush. Whoever the man was, he had no good knowledge of trailing, else when he lost the sorrel's tracks on the one side of the river, he would have crossed over and probed the opposite bank. It was evident he was unaware the stream could be forded at that point. That was probably fortunate, Chant decided, as he pressed on. He would as soon avoid any confrontations until he knew what was happening in the valley.

An hour later he topped out a low hill and saw the Gannon place in the distance. There'd been many improvements made—a new barn, several more corrals and holding pens, and the main house appeared to have been enlarged. That was not surprising. Tom Gannon was a good rancher and a smart one. He knew how to raise beef and had the all-important knack of always picking the exact time to market it when prices were at their best.

Cliff could do well, marrying into a family like the Gannons. Sarah—he remembered her only as a skinny kid with pigtails—hardly seemed old enough for marriage, but he reckoned she was at least eighteen now, perhaps a year more. Seemed strange—Cliff and Sarah becoming man and wife.

He reached the stone wall that framed the yard of the house and turned into the gate. Beyond the rambling structure, well clothed with vines to add coolness and bright with beds of flowers along its walls, he could see a man working around the corrals, another hoeing in a small garden plot. Everything looked well kept, orderly. It was not difficult to tell it was Tom Gannon's place.

He pulled up to the rack and halted. Immediately the screen door at the front of the house opened, and a girl stepped onto the porch. Slender, well built, sunlight glowing in her red-brown hair, she moved to the edge of the gallery and waited while he dismounted and crossed to her.

"Hello, Sarah," he said, removing his hat.

156

Surprise flared briefly in her hazel eyes, and then a quiet hostility crept into the features.

"So you've finally come," she murmured.

Dave Chant frowned. "You've been expecting me?"

"For five years . . . even longer."

He shook his head. "No reason to come back. Pa and Cliff were doing fine without me."

"Then why now?"

He shrugged, some of her hostility rubbing off onto him, turning him irritable. "Just took the notion."

"You know what's happened?"

"To Pa? Heard some of it. Not enough. Want to talk to Cliff about it. Understand he's here."

She studied him thoughtfully. Abruptly she spun and started for the door.

"I'll take you to him," she said.

VI

Dave followed the girl through the silent house, then suddenly recalled the amenities. "Your folks . . . they're all right?"

"Mama's dead. Two years ago," Sarah replied tonelessly. "Papa's out on the range somewhere."

"Sorry . . . about your mother," Chant murmured. "I didn't know, of course."

"Of course," she echoed in that same remote way.

Halting before the door at the end of the hall, she opened it and peeked in. "Asleep," she said in a low voice, and then pushed the panel aside for him to enter.

Shocked, Dave Chant halted in the center of the room. Cliff, the skin drawn tightly across the bones of his face, was almost unrecognizable. His arms were thin, and the outline of his body underneath a light coverlet was childlike.

"God in heaven!" Dave muttered hoarsely. "What . . . ?"

"Three bullets," Sarah replied. "He's been flat on his back in that bed for over two months."

"But why . . . ?" Chant began, and then checked himself.

Cliff's eyes had opened. He stared at Dave while a frown pulled at his wan features, and then suddenly his lips parted. His head came up as he made an effort to rise.

"Dave!"

Chant forced himself to smile. "Thought for a minute there you'd forgotten who I was," he said, moving forward and extending his hand.

"Forget? Not me!" Cliff said, taking his brother's fingers

158

into his own. "How long you been here?"

"Just rode in. Heard. . . ."

"Heard I was laid up," Cliff finished, "and that Pa was dead. Surprised you found out. From what I'm told nobody in town wants to talk about the Chants."

The bitterness in Cliff's voice was definite. Dave stepped back. "Seems to be some kind of a rule. It was old Heber told me where I'd find you."

"Heber. Always was a friend." Cliff paused momentarily, then said: "What brought you back?"

"Got an idea to drop by, see you and Pa. On my way to El Paso."

What he'd originally had in mind was without meaning now. Jared Chant was dead, and there was no more Box C, while Cliff. . . .

"Sorry Pa didn't get to see you before he died. Spoke of you pretty often during the last few years. You should have come home, Dave."

Chant's shoulders stirred. "Man does what he has to . . . what he thinks is best. Would've liked to see Pa, though." Abruptly he was tired of hedging, of the seemingly careful skirting of the facts. "What happened to you and Pa, Cliff?"

The younger Chant turned his head, stared out the window. A faint breeze was stirring the lace curtains that hung over the opening.

"We'll talk about Pa first," he said. "He was shot in the back. We found him on the trail to town. Dead."

"Marshal said he'd been robbed."

"Eighteen hundred dollars. He was taking it in to the bank to pay off a mortgage note."

"Mortgage!" Dave echoed. "Didn't know he had one."

"Couple of bad winters, few years back. Lost most of our herd. Pa took a loan to keep things going."

Dave considered that in silence. Finally he said: "Sloan said he wasn't able to run down the killer."

"Went through the motions. Turned up nothing."

Chant flung a keen glance at his brother. "Does that mean you don't think he tried very hard?"

"Oh, I reckon he did all he could. Just seemed to me like he wasn't working at it much. Jumped him about it. Claimed there wasn't anything he could do. You see, Pa lay there on the trail all night. If it was a drifter, he could have been fifty miles away before we found out what had happened. Marshal just figured it was too late to try doing anything."

"Besides, that kind of news wouldn't help the town any," Dave added dryly.

Cliff smiled wryly. "See you've been handed that line of bull, too."

"Only thing that seems important to Marshal Sloan is the reputation of Chamisa. Where'd he come from?"

"Texas somewheres. Fort Worth, I think. Been a lot of changes since you pulled out. Expect you saw that."

"Hardly know the place. Who owns the ranch now?"

"A man by the name of Barr . . . Andrew Barr. You probably saw that store he put up . . . the Emporium, he calls it."

"Saw it. . . . Thought you said Pa owed the bank. . . ."

"Did at the start. Seems Barr bought up the note. The man's got a lot of money and is doing a great deal of investing in the valley. Bringing in some of his friends from the East, too. Got them convinced this is where they can make a lot of cash."

That explained the appearance of Chamisa, the face lifting that had taken place. It also bore out Harry Sloan's overwhelming desire to keep all unsavory characters beyond the town's limits. It could lead to other answers. . . .

"This Barr . . . is he greedy enough to be back of Pa's killing?"

A fleeting look of shock crossed Cliff's face, and then he shook his head. "Maybe. I don't know. Not the first piece of property he's foreclosed on . . . and probably won't be the last."

"And he wouldn't be the first man to ever rig a deal where he could take over, either," Dave said acidly.

He was aware of Sarah's entry into the room. He hadn't been conscious of her leaving, so intently in conversation had he been with Cliff, but she was back now, bringing a tray upon which were a pot of coffee and two cups. Cliff watched her place the tray on a table near the head of the bed. He reached for her hand and smiled, a ragged, sorrowful grimace.

"Guess you hadn't heard Sarah and I had planned on getting married."

"Sure hadn't," Dave said, not wanting to spoil the moment for his brother. "Sounds like a fine idea. When's the big day?"

"When I'm back on my feet again," Cliff said. "Not before."

Sarah handed a half-filled cup of coffee to him, poured another for Dave. Her face was grave, and he thought he saw the glimmer of tears in her eyes as she turned to him.

"We don't have to wait," she said. "It's Cliff who. . . ."

"We'll wait," Cliff broke in firmly. "Hell, a man ought to be able to stand on his own two feet when he's up before the parson."

"Can't fault you there," Dave said, but he noticed that Sarah found no amusement in the light-hearted statement. "You ready to tell me how you got in such a shape?"

161

Cliff took a swallow of coffee, then set the cup on the tray. "Damned fool stunt . . . and my own doing. Barr sent the marshal and some of his own hired hands out to take over the Box C. Didn't hit me just right, somehow. Was only a couple of days after we'd buried Pa. Lost my head and grabbed up a scatter-gun. Couple of Barr's boys opened up on me."

"With the marshal right there with them?"

"He was there. Guess it happened so fast he couldn't stop them. Maybe a good idea he didn't. I'd have blasted a couple of them into kingdom come for sure, I was that fired up. Knew I had to give up the place, but like I said they come at me wrong."

"Sloan do anything about the shooting?"

"Not much he could do. Said I was in the wrong . . . actually resisting a lawful procedure, was the way he put it. The truth, too, I reckon, when you think it over."

"Expect so, only it seems to me the marshal goes a far piece out of his way to look after this Barr."

"Could be, but I never thought of it just that way. Lying here, I've done a lot of figuring, looking back. Can't see as there's anything that's happened to me, or to Pa, that wasn't the way it seems. Just took place, that's all. Nothing special about it."

"Probably right," Dave Chant said, but he was putting no belief in it—at least, not yet. Perhaps his association with men on the other side of the law provided him with a built-in skepticism when it came to situations such as the one he was encountering in the valley. It was a good trait to be trusting, to have faith in others, he supposed, but for himself he needed to be convinced.

Draining the last of the coffee, he placed the cup on the table and reached for Cliff's hand.

"Expect I've bothered you enough for one day. I'd best be moving along."

Disappointment clouded his brother's eyes. "You'll be back before you head out for El Paso?"

"Sure. I figured to hang around a couple of days. If you like, I'll drop back tomorrow."

"Be looking for you . . . Dave, glad you're not holding anything against me . . . well, for the way things were when you ran off."

"We were kids, then," Chant said. "Forgot all that a long time ago. . . . So long."

Turning, he followed Sarah back through the house. Halting on the porch, he laid his hand on the girl's shoulder and wheeled her around.

"I want the truth now. It happens I know a little about being shot up. Had a bullet or two dug out of my hide during the last few years. If this took place a couple of months ago, why's Cliff still lying there in that bed?"

Sarah's eyes filled quickly. She pulled away, lowered her head. Having a hard time controlling her voice, she said: "The doctor says there's a good chance Cliff'll never walk again."

VII

"Never walk again." Dave Chant repeated the words in a wooden voice. "Is it that bad?"

Sarah Gannon nodded. "Two of the bullets went into his hips, shattered the bones."

"Bones grow back. I've heard of. . . ."

"That's only a part of it. The doctor says a lot of Cliff's trouble is in his mind."

Chant stared at the girl. "You mean he doesn't want to get up out of that bed?"

"I don't understand it exactly," she said in a falling voice. "The way the doctor explains it, Cliff feels guilty about his . . . your pa's death. Thinks if he'd been with him that day it maybe wouldn't have happened."

"I wondered why he wasn't. That was a lot of money Pa was carrying."

Instantly she whirled on him. "You see! You know now why he feels guilty! Even you're blaming him."

"No," Chant said quietly, "I'm not. Just said I wondered."

"Well, Cliff wanted to ride in with him, but your pa wouldn't hear of it. Said he could look after himself. Cliff insisted, and your pa got real mad."

"Sounds like Pa, all right. Once he got his mind set, all hell wouldn't change it." Dave paused, then said: "You got any ideas about the murder . . . I mean other than what the marshal and everybody else seem to have made their minds up to?"

Sarah brushed at her eyes, pushed a stray wisp of hair

164

back from her face. "All I know is what I've been told . . . some outlaw did it for the money your pa was carrying."

"You don't think there's any connection with this man Barr foreclosing on the ranch?"

The girl frowned. "Don't see how. Andrew Barr is a rich man. Doubt if he'd stoop to killing to get something he probably didn't even want."

Dave mulled that over. "Don't quite know what you mean."

"He's got investments all around the country and that big store. Almost everybody trades with him. On top of that he apparently has more money than he knows what to do with. I'd think having to take over a ranch, foreclose, and be bothered with hiring people to run it would be about the last thing he'd want."

Chant shrugged. "Some men never get enough. I've known a few personally. Greed gets in their blood, and they start out to own the world . . . need it or not."

Sarah sighed heavily. "I guess it's possible, and maybe even true. But I don't care. I just wish there was something I could do for Cliff. Lying there in bed, he's just wasting away . . . dying, really, by inches."

"Don't give up yet," Chant said, stepping off the porch and moving toward the sorrel. "I aim to do a bit of digging. I could come up with something that will help."

She frowned. "You don't believe it happened the way they claim?"

He pulled the leathers free of the bar, swung to the saddle. "Let's just say I believe Pa was murdered, all right, but I'm not ready to accept it. Does that make any sense to you?"

For the first time, Sarah smiled. "No, it doesn't, but I'm glad you feel that way, Dave. Maybe you can do something

. . . help Cliff, give him hope."

"I'm promising nothing now, so don't build things up too high. It only just happens I'm not the trusting kind, and I need to look closer at a few things before I settle my mind. So long."

"Good bye," Sarah replied as he turned away.

Abruptly he pulled in. "Something I meant to ask but forgot. You know a man around here . . . big fellow, dark, with a scar on his face? Rides a bay gelding?"

"That's Con Wooton. Used to work for us. Works for Mister Barr now. Why?"

Con Wooton. Heber had mentioned him. Andrew Barr's bully boy. "Just wondered who he was. The valley's full of strangers, it seems," Dave said, and moved on.

But his thoughts did not stray from the man he'd discovered trailing him. Why would Wooton want to dog his tracks? How did the gunman know his identity? He hadn't been in the saloon when he'd asked about Cliff and his pa. Someone had carried the news of his presence to Barr's gun hawk plenty fast—someone who'd been in Kinsvater's. Or had it been Town Marshal Harry Sloan?

More questions crowded into Chant's mind. What business did the scar-faced Wooton have with him? Why would he take such sudden interest in his being in the valley? Dave felt his suspicions grow, strengthen. Wooton worked for Barr. Barr had foreclosed on the Box C when the note had not been met. It all tied in somehow—and now someone was anxious that he not probe too deeply into the affair. It had to be that, otherwise, Con Wooton would not have been keeping watch.

A rider on a white-legged black horse broke into view on a rise not far ahead. Chant's thoughts ended. He drew the sorrel down to a walk. Moments later he saw it to be Tom Gannon.

The rancher veered from his course and, pulling his rifle from its boot, assumed a diagonal that would enable him to intercept. Dave grinned. Everybody sure was touchy about strangers!

Gannon, frowning darkly under his wide-brimmed hat, stopped on a small knoll. "You're a hell of a long ways off the main road, mister," he called in a rough tone.

"For a fact," Chant replied, leaning forward. "How are you, Tom?"

The rancher stared. "Who the . . . Dave? Dave Chant . . . that you?"

"Sure enough," Chant answered, moving up and offering his hand.

Gannon smiled broadly, returned the rifle to its scabbard, and extended his own arm. "Never figured to see you around here again. Been out to see Cliff?"

"Coming from there now. Seems in a mighty bad way."

"Been a hell of a thing," Gannon said, wagging his head. "Jared getting bushwhacked, then Cliff losing the ranch and being shot up. Plenty reason for him to be feeling the way he does. What brought you back?"

"Took a notion to see Pa and Cliff again. Rode in this morning. Sure found things changed."

"Expect you did," the rancher said unsmilingly. "Everybody's got the fever. Chamisa's going to grow, be another Dalhart, they say. Maybe even another Denver."

"Could be . . . if this fellow Barr and your new town marshal have their way."

Gannon shifted in his saddle. "Appears you've met them."

"The badge toter, yes. Barr, no. Aim to look him up when I get to town."

"Barr? Why?"

167

"No special reason I can think of. Just aim to see what he's like . . . maybe ask a couple of questions."

"You wondering about your pa's killer?"

"A bit. You figure it's the way they say?"

"You mean something back of it besides robbery?"

Chant nodded slowly.

"No reason not to believe it," Gannon said. "Things like that happen. Man starts off with a lot of money on him. Somebody'd heard about it, waited along the trail, killed for it. Nothing new in that."

"No, guess not."

"Then why're you . . . ?"

"No use asking me why, because I plain don't know. But there's a burr sticking in me that I can't get rid of. Likely amounts to nothing, but before I ride on I've got to get myself satisfied." Chant paused, gazing off across the hills. "Could be nothing more than the way the marshal acted and talked. He was too anxious to keep me moving on. Somebody tries that on me, it always sets me to wondering why."

"I can answer that one for you," Gannon said with a laugh. "Sloan's afraid for his job. Barr and the other merchants have put it to him strong that unless he keeps a quiet town, they'll get somebody who can. Only reason he's so jumpy about a man like you riding in."

"He's jumpy, no doubt about that. The thing that bothers me is whether that's the real reason he's that way, or is there something else?"

"That's it," Gannon said confidently. "You can bet on it."

"Then why do you figure Barr's fancy gun thrower was trailing me this morning?"

"Wooton? You dead certain?"

"Sure as I know you're Tom Gannon. Somebody, and my guess is that it was the marshal, passed the word to him that I'd been around asking questions. This Wooton doesn't know me from Adam's off ox . . . leastwise, he didn't until today."

Gannon's eyes were on the ground. After a time he shook his head. "Makes no sense," he said. "Con works for Barr."

"That's what I'm getting at. If he was a deputy of Sloan's, I could understand it. It would mean the marshal was just keeping an eye on me. But being Barr's man. . . ."

"Andrew Barr's running this country," Gannon said, a note of bitterness in his voice. "No doubt of that. Could be he did send Wooton to watch you."

"If he did, he's got a reason . . . one I aim to get explained," Chant said, glancing to the sun now sliding toward Dead Horse Mesa. "Good seeing you, Tom. I'll look you up before I ride on."

Gannon said: "Sure. Drop by the place."

Dave touched the brim of his hat with a forefinger, then swung the sorrel away.

It was almost dark when Chant reached the outskirts of Chamisa and turned into the street. Locating a livery stable near the mid-point of the twin rows of buildings, he slanted the big red horse for it. Once he'd stabled the gelding, he would check into the Prairie Hotel, clean up, and have a good meal at one of the restaurants. There wasn't much else he could do now until morning.

He rode into the barn's runway, dismounted, and waited for a hostler to put in an appearance. The man arrived a few moments later, shambling up, sober-faced, from the murky depths of the building.

"Wasn't meaning to keep you standing, mister," he said. "Was busy helping fix up a friend of mine for burying."

Chant, in the process of removing his saddlebags, nodded. "No hurry. What happened? Your friend have some kind of an accident?"

The old man chafed his palms together, shook his head. "Weren't no accident," he said. "Somebody just pure beat Heber to death."

VIII

Chant wheeled slowly. "I hear you say Heber . . . the swamper over at Kinsvater's?"

The old man bobbed his head. "He's the one. Crippled-up fellow. Just can't figure somebody doing a thing like that. Heber never hurt nobody."

Dave was silent for a long minute. Heber had feared being seen, had made a point of caution. Who, specifically, had he been afraid of?

"Know what happened?"

"Reckon nobody knows for sure. Heber'd gone back out of the saloon to dump his sweepings. Didn't come back for a spell, so the bartender sent somebody to see what was keeping him. Found Heber in that old shed where they stack wood for wintertime. Stone dead . . . beat up something fierce."

Dave's thoughts were assembling hurriedly. Heber had mentioned Con Wooton, expressed a fear of the gunman. Later Dave had found Wooton trailing him. Did that add up to something?

"Reckon you were a pretty good friend of Heber's. Did he have any enemies? Ever hear him say anything about being threatened by somebody?"

The hostler's brows lifted. "You knew Heber?"

"From a long time back. Name's Chant."

The older man nodded. "Heard him mention the name. Far as somebody having it in for him, sure can't recollect him talking about it. Most folks liked him, felt sorry for him."

"What did the marshal say about it?"

"Nothing much. Couldn't find anybody who'd even seen Heber go into the shed or had noticed anybody hanging around it. Reckon he ain't got nothing to go on. Just one of them there things that happens."

"That the way the marshal said it?"

Again the hostler showed surprise. "Yeah, I guess maybe it was."

Harry Sloan had a pat answer to every situation, it seemed to Dave. Hanging his saddlebags over his shoulder, he reached into his pocket.

"I'd like to do my part in paying for a funeral," he said, producing several coins.

"No need. There's enough of us that knowed him close to look after things. Had a gold eagle on him, anyway. It'll satisfy the undertaker."

Chant nodded, walked the length of the runway to the door. Halting, he glanced up and down the street. Harry Sloan was speaking with a well-dressed man in front of the bank. A dozen or so more of Chamisa's residents were strolling along the sidewalk, enjoying the late evening coolness.

Crossing, he made his way to the Prairie Hotel, entered, and paused at the desk. The clerk, wordless, pushed the register and a stub of a pencil at him. Signing, Dave accepted the key, noted the number, and turned to the stairs. Only then did the balding man behind the counter break silence.

"Staying long?"

"Depends," Chant said, and continued up the short flight of steps.

The room was neat, clean, better than average. He guessed the spruce-up program in effect in Chamisa went deeper than just the surface. Washing down with the aid of the china bowl and pitcher, he shaved, drew on fresh clothing, and returned to the lobby.

"Where's the best place for a man to eat?" he asked, dropping his key on the counter.

"Next door," the clerk replied without troubling to look up.

The meal of steak and fried potatoes, fortified with hot biscuits, honey, and black coffee, was good, and, when it was finished, Chant remained at his table near the window, sipping a third cup of coffee and staring into the street with unseeing eyes while he thought about Heber and the brutal death that had overtaken the old man.

Again he wondered if the murder was in any way tied to the conversation he'd had with him. He had made certain no one was watching, just as Heber had requested, but there was, of course, no way he could be absolutely sure the by-play between them had not been witnessed. Someone at a second floor window might possibly have seen and guessed they were speaking. But it would have been only that—a guess. Dave knew he had used care, had not moved his head or made any motions.

But someone had gone into the shed and worked over the old, nearly helpless man so viciously that he had died from it. For what reason? Robbery had not been the cause. The gold piece he'd dropped into the dust for Heber had still been in his pocket when he was found. It appeared more logically to be an attempt to get information. What the hostler had said about Heber's not having any enemies was likely true. Inoffensive men such as the old swamper seldom did. They merely exist around a town, accepting handouts, living more or less on the charity of others and fearful always of rousing the ire of anyone.

Yes, there was a specific reason for Heber's death, and down deep in Dave Chant's mind a small voice cried out insistently that it had to do with him—with other things that were taking place in the valley. There was nothing to go on—nothing he could tie into. He grinned wryly. Those words sounded as if they'd come from Marshal Harry Sloan. But they were true. He couldn't let them stop him, however. Reaching out, grasping at smoke wisps, he concluded Heber could have been beaten to death by Con Wooton. The gunman had turned up on his trail not long after he'd talked with the old swamper.

Wooton could have been trying to force Heber to talk, tell to whom he had spoken, what had been said. It was possible—even probable. Certainly someone had put Con Wooton onto him. Why?

That was the all-important question. Why had the gunman trailed him? The answer was simple. Someone had something to hide and didn't want him prowling around, turning up some hidden secret that could change things in the town—in the valley. Who would that someone be?

Wooton worked for Andrew Barr. It was only natural to assume that Barr was the darkness that feared the light. Harry Sloan seemed only a side issue, afraid, as Tom Gannon had said, for his job. But it could go deeper as far as the lawman was concerned. He could be working right along with Barr, just as Con Wooton would be doing. This would not be unusual. Many a lawman, knowing which side of his bread the butter was spread on, rode boot in stirrup with the lawless.

He was close to the answer, Dave felt with satisfaction— or, at least, a key to it. Just how far-reaching the connections were, he could only guess. But it was entirely possible that Jared Chant had been killed not for his money, but to prevent his paying off the note that would have saved his ranch. Turned grim by the thought, Dave rose, dropped a silver dollar onto the table to pay for his check and tip the waitress, and made his way to the door.

All he had were guesses, hunches—and a conviction that all was not the way he was supposed to believe. But he'd ridden that road before. There was a stubbornness in him that would not be put off, pushed aside so easily, as had been the case with Cliff and Tom Gannon and maybe a few others in the valley. He would have to know in his own mind that Jared Chant had been murdered for his money, that nothing more lay behind the crime, and the best place to start convincing himself of one or the other was with the man from whom all things seemed to flow—Andrew Barr.

Stepping out onto the café landing, he threw his glance toward the Emporium. Lights shone brightly in all windows. Barr would still be there. Turning, he started down the plank walk.

Immediately a figure stirred in the darkness blanketing the passageway alongside the hotel. Chant felt the hard muzzle of a pistol jab into his spine, heard a low voice rasp into his ear.

"You're comin' with us, cowboy."

IX

Chant froze. A short distance down the street Marshal Harry Sloan was watching intently. Others along the walks seemed not to notice.

"Move, god damn you," a second voice commanded from the deep shadows.

The gun muzzle dug sharper. Dave turned into the blackness of the littered corridor, seeing in that same moment Harry Sloan wheel deliberately, placing his back to the scene and strolling off.

Cursing silently, Chant moved on under the pressure of the weapon against his spine. A third shape loomed up in the murk. Three of them. They were taking no chances with him, it would seem. Who were they?

They reached the end of the passageway and broke out into a vacant lot behind the restaurant and next to the Prairie Hotel's stable. Faint light from the weak moon illuminated his captors somewhat now, and Dave gave them hurried appraisal.

One was the rider he'd encountered at the Bar C earlier that day. The two others he'd never seen before. Were they pals of the first man, out to help their friend get even for the belt he'd taken at the ranch? But the meaning could go deeper.

He felt a hand claw at his holster, was conscious of the lightening at his hip as his pistol was yanked free. Hands grabbed at his arms and pinned them back. Abruptly he found himself imprisoned by two of the men, held helpless between them.

176

"Here you go, Curly. He's all yours," one said.

Chant saw the dark figure of Curly surge toward him. He twisted, took a shocking blow to the ribs.

"Hold him, dammit!" the rider snapped, and struck again.

Dave grunted as the cowpuncher's fist drove into his belly. His senses reeled as a quick follow-up blow caught him on the side of the head. He jerked hard, struggled to pull away, to break the tight grasp upon his arms being maintained by Curly's two friends.

"Learning me manners, you was saying?" the cowpuncher snarled. "I'll learn you a thing or two!"

Another blow smashed into Chant's middle. He sagged, wind bursting from his lips in a gusty sound, and stumbled as his right foot became entangled with one of those of his captors. Instantly he raised his leg and stomped hard. The heel of his boot came down solidly on someone's instep. A yell of pain went up, and the hold on his right arm slackened.

Dave lunged to the opposite side, throwing his weight against the cowpuncher to his left, and broke clear. The other, off balance, went stumbling backward. Chant, pressing his advantage, charged into the rider and went crashing to the ground with him. Free, thoroughly aroused, Dave Chant was on his feet instantly, aware of Curly's shouts, of the sound of the man rushing in to drive him down again. He dodged to one side, whirled, caught the rider by the shoulder, and shoved hard.

Curly went sprawling across the body of his friend, who at that moment was struggling to rise. Both collapsed in a tangle of legs and arms, cursing wildly. Chant leaped over the threshing bodies, scooped up his pistol from where it had fallen. Jamming it into its holster, he wheeled to meet the first of Curly's helpers, on his feet and moving in. Stepping quickly to his left, Chant swung a quick blow, stalled the man. Instantly he crossed with a right that cracked like a whip when it connected with the cowpuncher's jaw. The man dropped soundlessly.

Dave was moving away before the cowpuncher was fully down. In the dust-filled dimness he saw Curly pulling himself upright, crouching, hand fumbling for the pistol at his hip.

Chant lashed out with a booted foot, caught Curly on the forearm. The cowpuncher yelled and tried to back away as the weapon flew off into the darkness. Once more he collided with the third man, who was again endeavoring to rise.

"God dammit . . . quit running into me!" the rider growled, going down once more.

Dave rushed in. He reached for Curly, caught him by the arm, spun him half around. Swinging hard, he smashed a right to the jaw. Curly's knees buckled. Chant, cool and methodical, hammered a left to the man's middle, and followed with a crackling drive to the ear. Curly's legs gave way. He began to sink, head forward, arms dangling loosely at his sides.

Chant stepped back, eyes on the last of the three. The man had given up trying to rise and now simply sat in the dust. Dave crossed to him.

"What about it?" he demanded, the words coming out tightly between labored breathing.

"Count me out," the cowpuncher said quickly. "Ain't no fight of mine. Was all Curly's."

Chant eased back a step. An earlier suspicion-filled thought recurred to him. "Curly . . . and who else?"

The rider stared up at him. "Don't know nothing about

nobody else. Curly said he aimed to square up for that whopping you gave him this morning. Asked Buck and me to side him."

Chant made a threatening move. The cowpuncher threw up an arm, cringing. "That's the truth, so help me! Iffen somebody else was in on it, I sure don't know nothing about it!"

"You work for Barr, same as Curly does."

"Lots of us working for Barr. Don't ever see him, howsomever. Pete Hawley's our boss . . . does the ramrodding for him."

"Thought Con Wooton held down that job."

"Naw, he just sort of hangs around Mister Barr. Runs errands and does chores for him. Don't have nothing to do with the ranching end of it, 'cepting he sleeps out at the place."

The rider was telling the truth, most likely. Curly could have been out to even the score and enlisted the aid of a couple of friends. It would be a natural thing for a cowpuncher to do. Shrugging, Dave moved off a few steps. He'd been suspicious at first, particularly when he'd seen the town lawman turn away, deliberately ignoring what was plainly the beginning of trouble. He'd have a few things to say to Harry Sloan about that.

"All right," Chant said. "I'm believing you." He pointed to Curly, who was now stirring feebly. "Tell him, when he wakes up, I'll still be around if he wants to try teaching me that lesson again."

The cowpuncher made no reply, simply stared. Dave stooped, recovered his hat, and employed it to dust off his clothing.

"This ramrod you were talking about . . . Pete Hawley. What's he look like?"

"Like anybody else, I reckon."

"Covers a lot of ground."

"About your size. Wears himself a full mustache."

Chant shook his head. "Reckon I haven't run across him yet."

"Ain't likely to. Keeps busy trotting around looking after Mister Barr's ranches."

Dave's attention settled on that. "How many spreads this Barr own?"

"Half a dozen . . . maybe more. Ain't never made it my business to find out."

"Seems he's done right well in this country," Chant said, turning toward the passageway. "Makes a man wonder how."

It was something he'd find out later. At the moment he wanted a few words with Marshal Harry Sloan.

X

Chant reached the sidewalk and halted. Anger was building within him now as he threw a sharp glance down the street to the point where he'd last seen the lawman. There was no sign of Harry Sloan.

Immediately he strode into the center of the dusty roadway, bent his steps in that direction. Sloan would be somewhere along the route. Moving fast, he came abreast of the marshal's office. It was deserted. He continued, eyes shifting back and forth. A small sigh of satisfaction escaped his tight lips. Two men stood in the shadows fronting the bank. One was Aaron Faber, the other was Sloan.

Angling through the loose dust, Dave pulled up before the two men. Faber looked at him closely, and then lowered his head. Sloan greeted him with a lazy smile.

"Looks like you had yourself a bit of a tussle. Bound to come, way you been strutting around. Ready now to move on?"

"Not by a damned sight!" Chant snapped. "You saw what was happening. If you're so set on keeping this town full of law and order, why didn't you step in?"

"Nothing wrong in a couple of the boys blowing off a little steam."

"That all it was?"

Sloan's features hardened. "Meaning what?"

"Are you sure Curly and his two *compadres* weren't sent in to work me over by your friend Barr?"

"Now, hold on, Chant. . . ."

"Your walking off, making no move to stop it, looks a

mite funny to me. My guess is you knew what it was all about, and stayed clear."

Sloan's answer was cool. "You go ahead, do all the guessing you want."

"Appears to be your favorite pastime . . . guessing. Like Heber. I suppose it was a drifter that beat him to death."

"I'm looking into it."

"Anyway, that little stunt in the alley didn't work. Curly and his friends got a bit more than they bargained for. As for me moving on . . . no chance."

Harry Sloan shrugged. "You're a fool, Chant. Ought to see by now that you're following a blind trail."

"Hardly. Every time I turn around, I get a stronger hunch that I'm not. Something stinks about this whole thing, and I figure I'd best hang around until I find out what it is."

"Marshal," Faber said hesitantly, "I expect I'd better run along. Supper's waiting, and I. . . ."

"Not before you answer a couple of questions," Dave cut in sharply.

The banker frowned, looked quickly at the lawman, and then back to Chant. "Questions? About your pa's death? Nothing I can tell you."

"Pa was coming in to pay off that note he owed you. . . ."

"Owed Mister Barr. The bank was only acting as a collection agent."

"I heard. You sure turned out to be a good friend of Pa's . . . selling him out without telling him."

"I conduct the bank's business in what I consider best for the interests of the stockholders," Faber said starchily.

"Seems you do, and old friends be damned."

"Just a minute here!" Sloan protested. "You've got no call. . . ."

"Who all knew Pa was bringing in that money?" Dave continued, ignoring the lawman.

Faber frowned again. "Well, can't say as I can answer that. My clerk, of course. And Mister Barr. Don't recall ever talking about it in front of anybody in particular other than them."

"Do a little hard thinking," Chant said.

The banker rubbed his chin. "Might have come up some time or other. You're asking me to do something that's nigh impossible . . . and I sure wouldn't know who your pa mentioned it to."

"He wouldn't have told anybody. He had too much pride to admit he owed you anything."

Faber stirred restlessly. "Well, I wish I could help you, but there's nothing I can say." He hesitated, then added: "I'm sorry the way matters turned out for you and your family. And I wouldn't have sold that note if I hadn't been forced."

"Can't see as it would've made any difference," Sloan said. "He'd still have been bringing in the money, and the hold-up would've happened no matter who held the note."

Chant had to agree. He nodded to Faber. "You keep thinking about it. Maybe you'll remember who you did some talking in front of."

"But the marshal figures. . . ."

"Forget him," Dave said bluntly. "He may be satisfied, but I'm not. Be dropping around to see you again in a day or so. Try having some names for me."

Harry Sloan's face had tightened, changed to a deeper hue. "Just who the hell do you think you are . . . coming in here, taking over?"

"I'm the son of the man who got murdered and the brother of the boy lying out at Gannon's shot up so bad he may never walk again," Dave rasped angrily. "And I'm not about to look the other way when I think there's something haywire!"

"You've got no reason to think that," Sloan replied, again in control of his temper. "All you're going on is a fool hunch."

"Something I never ignore. And the way things are around here, the one I've got gets stronger every minute."

"Smart thing for you to do is forget it," the lawman said. "You won't turn up nothing but trouble for yourself. You ain't forgetting I warned you?"

"I'm not. Could have used my gun back there when your three friends jumped me."

"Nothing says I can't send out them telegrams, either."

Anger flared through Dave Chant. "You do that, Marshal," he said tautly, "and you've got some real trouble on your hands!"

"That a threat?"

"A promise. I'm aiming to do my looking around quiet-like, but if you try stopping me, I'll take back my word and handle things any way I see fit. That clear?"

Sloan was silent for a long minute. Then he said: "I won't have you stirring up my town over a killing for no good reason, either. That clear to you?"

"I've got good reason. Maybe you can't see it, but I can. Now, if that doesn't set with you, go right ahead and pop your whip."

"Can't see as it would do any harm, Harry," Faber said. "I expect he's within his rights."

"He's got no right prying into other people's business, getting them upset."

"No cause for them to get upset if they've nothing to hide," Dave said, eyes narrowing.

"Don't mean there is anything to hide. Just that this thing was settled once, and everybody was satisfied. I'm sorry about your pa and your brother. So's the rest of the folks around here. But it's a closed matter, and no good'll come of opening the sore again."

Chant's glance was still pressing the lawman. "You wouldn't be fretting about what I might turn up, would you, Marshal?"

"Hell, no, I ain't. Just happens I'm trying to keep this town quiet . . . decent."

"Sure, so's it'll grow and all the people'll get fat and rich. You've already sung that song. Well, I don't give a damn about your town and the people in it. I've got some questions in mind that are hollering for answers. I'm going to get them."

Abruptly Chant wheeled, started to move away. Harry Sloan came to quick attention. "Where do you think you're heading?"

"Down the street . . . to talk to Andrew Barr."

Sloan's features became dark again. "You stay away from him! I won't have you bothering. . . ."

Chant came to a full halt. "You figure to stop me, Marshal?" he asked, his tone a soft challenge.

In the hush that followed, the sounds of the night seemed loud, magnified. Finally Sloan shrugged. "Suit yourself," he murmured, and swung about.

XI

Barr's Emporium was a store of considerable proportions and well stocked with merchandise of all kinds, Dave noted as he walked through the wide doorway and stopped just inside. Racks of clothing, shelves filled with every conceivable article—it was a general store on a grand scale. But at the moment only three customers were to be seen moving among the displays.

A young male clerk bustled forward and bowed slightly to Dave. "Anything special I can do for you, sir?"

"You can tell me where Andrew Barr is," Chant replied.

The clerk glanced over his shoulder to a door at the rear of the wide room marked **PRIVATE**. "Not sure he's in," he said uncertainly.

"Reckon I'll see," Dave said, and brushed on by the younger man.

"Wait. I ought to. . . ."

Ignoring the protest, Chant walked the distance through the welter of counters and racks. Halting at the door, he knocked once, then pushed the panel open.

A balding, red-faced man with a cigar clenched between his teeth sat at a massive roll-top desk placed against a side wall. He swung half around at Dave's entrance and stared irritably.

"Come right in," he said dryly.

Chant bobbed his head, moved deeper into the room. Suddenly he was conscious of the presence of others—two men. They were slouched in chairs against the wall behind the door. One was the scar-faced individual who'd trailed him—Con Wooton. The other he'd never seen before, a big man with a thick mustache.

"What can I do for you?" the balding man at the desk asked briskly.

Chant, easing about until he had all three before him, said: "You Andrew Barr?"

"I am."

"Name's Chant. Couple of questions I'm here to ask."

Barr exhaled a cloud of smoke. "Concerning what?"

"Murder of my pa, Jared Chant."

The merchant leaned back in his swivel chair, studying Dave narrowly. "You the other son?"

Chant nodded. "One your boys didn't get a chance to work over."

Barr frowned and shook his head. "Don't know what you're talking about. And your pa . . . well, I don't know anything about that, either. Only what I've been told."

"Nobody seems to know much about it," Dave said. "That's one of the things that's bothering me."

"I leave matters such as that to the law," Barr said. "What was it you wanted to ask?"

Chant glanced to the men sitting along the wall. Evidently Andrew Barr didn't think an introduction was necessary. He misread Dave's look.

"Go ahead, you can talk in front of them. They work for me."

Chant pushed the point. "Don't think I know either one . . . not exactly, anyway."

Barr waved a heavy hand at the pair. "Pete Hawley, my ranch foreman . . . or ramrod, as you call him down in this part of the country. Con Wooton . . . well, he's sort of a . . . a handy man."

Chant grinned, nodded to both. "I see."

"Now, what do you want? I'm a little busy."

"One thing special . . . who knew my pa was bringing in that money to pay off the note on his place?"

Barr's face was puzzled. "How'd I know that?"

"You could've mentioned it."

"Maybe I did. It would be hard to remember anything like that. I've got a lot of investments around here. I talk about them now and then."

Chant shifted his attention to Wooton. "Did you know about it?"

The scar-faced man returned Dave's glance coolly. "Maybe I did, maybe I didn't. Don't recollect."

Dave passed on to Hawley. "You?"

The ranch foreman shrugged. "Can't remember ever hearing Mister Barr mention it. It's possible, though."

"What difference does it make?" Barr asked.

"Could make plenty. If somebody knew he was carrying all that cash and waited for him, they would have had to learn it from you . . . or Faber, the banker."

"I suppose so," the merchant said quietly. "But Marshal Sloan seemed to think it was some drifter . . . just an ordinary hold-up."

"Sloan takes the easy way out when he's up against a problem. That was a side road my pa was riding that day. Not much more'n a trail. There'd be no drifters on it."

Barr considered that, stirred impatiently. "Well, you could be right, but I don't see how I can help you any. My business is running this store and looking after the investments I make, not trying to be a lawman."

"Was this the first time somebody who owed you got robbed on the way in to pay you off?"

The merchant flushed hotly. "Are you implying that I . . . ?"

"Just a question, that's all. I'd like to have your answer."

"It was. There'd been no trouble like this before. And if you're trying to say. . . ."

"Not trying to say anything, Barr. Just asking a question. My pa was murdered . . . and not by some drifter. I'll lay odds on that."

Andrew Barr picked up the pencil he'd been using and studied its point. "Well, if you're sure, then I expect you've got reasons. I'm sorry about it . . . sorry about what happened to your brother, too, but with me business is business. The mortgage note wasn't paid. I had to foreclose regardless of circumstances. Now, if you're finished. . . ."

"He's finished," Con Wooton said, coming to his feet and facing Chant. "Move on, mister. You're wasting the boss' time."

Dave studied the gunman quietly. Barr raised his hand. "Never mind, Con."

The scarred gunman did not move for a long breath, and then he settled back into his chair. Dave had a passing inclination to call Wooton's hand, let him know he'd seen him on the trail that morning, but he decided against it. It was something he'd hold in reserve until later.

"Is there anything else?"

Chant came back to the merchant. "That about covers it. If I think of anything, I'll be back."

"Don't bother," Barr said, turning again to his desk. "Take it up with the marshal. There's nothing I can tell you that you don't already know."

"I doubt that," Chant said, and, wheeling, he returned to the sidewalk.

He stood for a full minute, eyes on the deserted street, considering what he had learned. Very little, if anything, of value, he was forced to admit. But he'd not expected to turn up much. It had been more of a move calculated to stir up embers, start the killer, if he was actually still around, to worrying and possibly making a move.

Also, he had wanted to have a look at Andrew Barr, the man who had virtually taken over the valley. That he was all business there was no doubt. It was not difficult to understand how he had made himself a wealthy man. The question it posed was immediate—could Barr be ruthless enough to use murder as a means for increasing his wealth? Could he have had Jared Chant bushwhacked to prevent him from paying off the mortgage on the Box C?

That likelihood tugged at Dave Chant's mind as he moved off the porch and crossed the street to walk on the opposite side. It was worth investigating further. He'd find out how many other places Andrew Barr had taken over, look into the circumstances. . . .

The sharp, flat crack of a gunshot shattered the stillness of the night. Glass in a window directly behind Chant shattered as the bullet, missing its target by inches, smashed into the dusty pane.

Instantly Dave dropped low, ducked into a wood-filled passageway alongside the building he was passing. In the deep shadows he crouched, searched the line of structures across the street for signs of the hidden marksman. He could see no movement.

Lights were blossoming in several windows. A man had come into the open farther down—Harry Sloan. Beyond him someone was yelling questions. The lawman, ignoring the shouts, was approaching at a fast walk.

Cautious, Chant doubled back along the passageway, circled the adjacent building, and returned to the street a short distance below the point where the bullet had almost struck him. If the bushwhacker yet waited, he'd offer him no second opportunity.

Reaching the sidewalk, he halted in the darkness. Sloan, almost abreast, pulled up short, pivoted, and came to him.

"Might've known!" the lawman raged. "Something like this was bound to come!"

Chant smiled. "Not what you've been trying to make me believe, Marshal. You claim the killer was a drifter, not somebody around here."

"Still say it was."

"Then why do you figure somebody would take a shot at me?"

"Mainly because you're who you are . . . and because you're nosing around, stirring up trouble."

Chant shook his head. "You'll have to do better than that."

"I don't have to do nothing but keep things quiet around here," Sloan snapped. "And that's what I'm going to do. . . . Mister, I want you gone from here by tomorrow!"

Chant's head came up slowly. "You ordering me out of town?"

"That's what I'm doing."

"It seems to me you're chasing out the wrong man. Why not find out who threw that lead at me . . . run him off?"

"You heard me! Saddle up and be on your way by sunrise."

Chant's shoulders stirred. "Whatever you say," he murmured, and moved on toward the hotel.

But leaving Chamisa was far from his plans now. He'd pull out of town just to keep the marshal quiet and from underfoot—but he'd not go far. The embers he'd fanned were apparently getting hot in the right places.

XII

Shortly after sunup the next morning Dave Chant, saddle-bags slung over his shoulder, came from the lobby of the Prairie Hotel. Halting on the porch, he glanced toward the marshal's office. Harry Sloan stood in the doorway, face turned toward him. Chant gave no sign of greeting, simply wheeled and entered the nearby restaurant.

He ate a large breakfast at a leisurely pace, enjoying a second and a third cup of coffee, paid his check, and re-traced his steps to the street. Sloan had not moved from the entrance to his quarters. Scarcely noticing the lawman, Chant then walked to the livery stable and began to saddle the sorrel.

The old hostler with whom he'd spoken the previous day, roused from his cot, came forward sleepily to help out and collect his fee. Dave waited until the big red was ready and then, procuring a coin from his pocket, paid the sorrel's bill.

"Anything new on Heber's killer?" he asked, swinging onto the saddle.

The hostler yawned, shaking his head. "Nothing. Reckon the marshal ain't bothering much."

"You mean he's not trying at all?"

"Oh, I guess he's been asking questions around. Ain't learned nothing he didn't already know. He figures Heber didn't count for much, I suspect, and there ain't no use working at it too hard. Besides, he don't like for things like that to get bandied about. Says it hurts the town."

"Does a lot of worrying about keeping the lid on around

192

here, it seems. Real public-spirited man."

The old man nodded slowly. "You hear that shot last night?"

"Down near the Emporium? Sure did."

"Been wondering what it was all about. Bet it riled the marshal right smart."

"No doubt," Chant said. "Anybody ride in about that time . . . or ride out?"

The older man clawed at his matted beard. "Nope, don't recollect seeing anybody. Why? Would it have something to do with that shooting?"

"Could have," Dave replied, and, wheeling the sorrel around, rode down the runway and into the street.

Harry Sloan was still there, slouched against the frame of his door. Chant deliberately headed for the lawman, picking a course in the center of the roadway. When he passed the lawman, he touched the brim of his hat with a forefinger.

"*Adiós,* Marshal," he said.

Sloan made no answer, but there was an angry flush on his cheeks and a hard set to his mouth. He'd be satisfied now. He'd let the matter drop, and Dave felt he'd get no more opposition from the lawman as long as he stayed clear of the settlement—which was fine with him. All else would come—if it was to come—somewhere out on the range.

He glanced to the Emporium, to the buildings lying to the north of it along the street. From some point, the hidden marksman had fired his bullet, missing, luckily, and doing no more damage than breaking the window of the Bon Ton Shoe & Boot Repair Shop. Whoever it was had meant to kill him, he was sure of that, and chances were better than good that it was the same man who'd bush-whacked his father—notwithstanding Harry Sloan's reasons and contentions to the contrary. He was getting close, treading on somebody's toes, and it would have been a good idea to close in after that shot had been fired, trying to flush whoever it was out of the shadows. But it wouldn't have been a very practical thing to do—not with the killer holding all the aces at that moment. Likely he would never have made it across the street. Harry Sloan barging in when he did had ruined the opportunity, anyway.

Who could it have been? Con Wooton? Pete Hawley? Andrew Barr himself? Any one of the three, by moving fast, could have left the Emporium by a rear exit, hurried down the alley paralleling the street for a short distance, and laid in wait until Dave had drawn abreast. It could easily have been any one of them, or it could be someone else, someone who'd watched him enter Barr's store and hung around in the shadows until he came out. If that were true, then it was someone he'd given no consideration to at all.

He thought of Curly and the two who'd jumped him earlier. Immediately he ruled them out. They weren't killers, only brawlers, and, although Curly's peeve might be stronger now than ever, he wasn't the sort to settle a grudge with a gun. He'd get his satisfaction with his fists—or try to, anyway. It could be anyone, someone he knew or a perfect stranger, a Johnny-Come-Lately to the valley. There was no way of knowing, but one thing was certain—he'd got uncomfortably close, so close, in fact, that the killer had made a try for him and missed. That miss was what counted, and, when Harry Sloan had delivered his ultimatum there in the street afterward, Chant had already been thinking, planning, and thus offered no opposition. The killer would follow, would seek him out to make good the shot that had failed. Thus he would tip his hand. Things were working out much better than Dave had hoped.

Reaching the end of the street, Chant cut west, striking

for the low, bubble-like sand hills and buttes that bordered the lower end of the valley. He had no definite scheme in mind other than the public departure from Chamisa, which he felt certain would be witnessed by the bushwhacker. He could swing over to Tom Gannon's Triple X, bunk there with the hands, but that meant seeing Cliff again, and he wasn't quite up to that. Looking at his brother lying helpless did something to him. It made him think of the years he'd lost, years when he could have been home pulling his share of the load on the ranch. It brought back a flood of memories, too, good and bad, all of which disturbed him more than he cared to admit.

There was Sarah, too, grown now into a beautiful young woman. Had he remained on the ranch, Sarah might have been his rather than Cliff's. Maybe not. Maybe she would have preferred Cliff regardless, but at least he would have had his chance with her. Now she looked upon him with something close to scorn, even distaste, in her eyes and hated what she knew him to be. She was wrong in a lot of her thinking. Stories always sprang up about a man who lived by his gun. Exaggeration was easy, and there were those who built legends for the sheer joy of being listened to. Men were seldom as bad or as good as they were portrayed by others. It was only that the recounting of their activities was all too often blown up and reached proportions well beyond reason. Maybe, before this was done with, he could change Sarah's ideas about him a little. Maybe he could show her there could be some good in what she considered wholly bad. It was something to try for.

He slowed the sorrel, the faint *thud* of a horse on the trail behind him claiming his attention. A hard grin cracked his lips. That chance to show Sarah might come sooner than he hoped, he thought, swinging off the trail into a narrow gully to

195

his left. If the killer proved to be connected with Andrew Barr, the possibility of getting the Bar C back for Cliff—the very best medicine possible for his recovery—would be good.

It was Harry Sloan.

Chant, cursing softly, watched the lawman round the end of the butte, halt the buckskin he rode, rise in the stirrups, and look out over the range, puzzled.

"Right here, Marshal!" Dave called in a quiet voice.

Sloan, startled, wheeled sharply. Anger and confusion mottled his features. "Why the hell . . . ?"

"Taking a long chance," Dave continued, moving out of the draw. "The way things are around here you could have caught yourself a bullet. Are you trailing me?"

"Having myself a look," Sloan replied.

"Little off your stomping grounds. The way I understand it, your job ends at the town limits."

"Anything that has to do with my town is where I go!" the lawman snapped.

Chant nodded coldly. "Fair enough, Marshal, but don't include me in that kind of figuring. And I'm getting a bellyful of being trailed. The next man trying it's likely to find himself with a bullet in his hide."

Wheeling the sorrel about, Chant rode off, striking deeper into the hills. A quarter hour later he looked back. Harry Sloan was on his way back to town. Dave shrugged. The lawman had been curious, he guessed, had simply ridden out to see where he had gone. Sloan was that kind— a town marshal wanting to keep his finger on everything. A man might think Sloan would have done a better job in trying to run down Jared Chant's killer instead of just brushing lightly over the surface and then striving to hush up the whole affair. That is, unless the lawman was working with the person who'd actually done the killing or had some connection with him.

Dave mulled that over as he rode on. Could Sloan be working with Andrew Barr—assuming Barr was behind the murder? Was that the reason the lawman was so eager to keep everything quiet in the settlement and had actually forbidden Dave to make a call on the merchant? Or was he truly sincere in his claim to want a decent town, a good place to which people could come? It was hard to figure, and Harry Sloan was harder yet to figure out. He guessed only time and events would bring the answers.

On a hill not far south of the Box C's buildings Chant pulled to a stop, still undecided what his best move should be. For the second time, Sloan had spoiled his play—his hope that the killer would follow when he rode out of Chamisa. He needed now to come up with another idea, a plan whereby, using himself as bait again, he could draw the ambusher from hiding.

The Box C. That seemed a logical place to start. Go there, have a look around, let himself be seen by someone other than Curly and his two friends. If he were stopped, he could explain that he had once lived there, that he simply wanted to visit the old place before he moved on. It was too late to profess ignorance of the ranch's change in owner-ship. Someone—Heber he thought it was—had said Barr's men all hung out at the Box C. That would mean Wooton and Pete Hawley, too. If the killer was not one of the ob-vious suspects, he might in some way tip his hand.

It was worth the try. Dangerous, perhaps, but hell, it was dangerous even to ride down the valley, the way things stacked up, and he had to do something, since Harry Sloan had messed up what had been his best bet. As that thought occurred to him, a rifle bullet came racing out of the dis-tance, grazed him, sent him tumbling to the sand.

XIII

Stunned but conscious, Dave Chant lay face down on the warm earth. A burning sensation traced a course along the side of his head, keeping company with an intense throb of pain. As his senses returned quickly to normal, he became aware of oncoming horses, pounding up fast. Closing his eyes, he remained motionless.

Two men. He heard them pull up, heard the *thud* of their boot heels as they came off their saddles, trotted to where he lay.

"You sure did nail him," a voice said. "Got him right smack in the head."

"I wasn't exactly aiming to do that. I was only wanting to put a bullet through his hat, give him a scare."

"Sure, sure. Since when'd you get all that good at shooting?"

There was a long minute of silence. Finally the first voice said: "Well, he's your punkin, Gabe. What're you going to do with him?"

"Can't leave him laying here, for certain," Gabe replied. "Who you reckon he is?"

"Search me . . . some saddle bum would be my guess."

Dave felt a hand grip his shoulder, pull, roll him onto his back. Gabe swore in surprise.

"Hell, Earl . . . it's that jasper Curly tangled with!"

"And he sure ain't dead. He's breathing."

Instantly Gabe's hand thrust itself under Chant's shirt, probed for a heartbeat. "Just knocked him out, that's all," the cowpuncher said in a relieved voice. "Only creased him."

198

"That's lucky for you," Earl said. "You know how Hawley feels about shootings. Still got to figure what to do with him, howsomever."

"Ain't nothing to do 'cepting tote him in to the ranch. Can't leave him laying out here for the coyotes."

"What about Hawley?"

"Just have to own up to it. Man don't hardly know what he's to do on this dang' job anyway. Hawley says don't do no shooting. Con Wooton says shoot to kill. Somebody ought to make up somebody's mind so's a man would know. . . ."

"Hawley's running the ranch. He's the one we better be listening to."

"But Con's working right out of the old bear's den . . . and he ain't the one to cross. Catch up that sorrel, Earl, and help me load this bird on the saddle."

Feigning unconsciousness, Chant allowed himself to be hoisted onto his horse. At first he had sworn inwardly at having his plans once again disrupted, this time by accident, but now the situation could prove to be a lucky break—although coming the hard way. He'd be able to get into the Box C, perhaps pick up stray bits of information that might prove helpful. It was of doubtful value, but already he had learned something—there was friction between Pete Hawley and Barr's gunman, Con Wooton—and it would appear Wooton was not liked.

It was an uncomfortable ride, if a short one, draped over the saddle as he was, and Chant heaved a sigh of relief when he saw the hard-packed ground of the yard beneath the sorrel's hoofs and heard sounds of activity. Two more men came trotting up when the party halted before the hitch rack at the rear of the house, both shouting questions.

"Got me a trespasser," Gabe explained.

"Accidental-like," Earl added. "Take a hold, you boys. Lug him into the house, where Cookie can do some doctoring on him."

"One of you had better take that there iron of his'n," a new voice said. "He's going to be roaring mad once he comes to."

Chant felt himself being dragged off the saddle. Hands gripped him under the armpits, by the legs. Cracking his eyelids cautiously, he tried to get a look at the men carrying him into the house. He could see only the one holding his legs—a squat, bearded old cowpuncher who was having a hard time keeping up.

They entered the building, passed through the kitchen where the odor of simmering stew and coffee laid a strong odor, down the short hallway Dave remembered well, and into one of the back bedrooms where several cots had been placed.

"Put him there by the window so's I can see what I'm doing."

Chant realized he could not hope to keep up the pretense much longer, but perhaps he could stall for a while. As they laid him down, he groaned, opened his eyes. A graying old man with a stubble of beard was bending over him.

"Well, he ain't dead," he announced, pulling the cork from a bottle he was holding.

"Knowed that when we brought him in," Gabe said.

The cook grunted. Taking a cloth pad, he soaked it with fluid from the bottle, began to dab at the wound on Chant's head. Dave groaned again, jerked away.

"Burns like hell's fire, don't it, son?" the cook said, grinning maliciously. He straightened up. "He ain't scarcely hurt none. Who is he?"

"Don't know, 'cepting he's the one Curly and the others had the ruckus with in town."

The cook's lips pursed into a soundless whistle. "Do tell! He looks like he might be a real he-cat, all right."

"What're you aiming to do with him?" asked one of the cowpunchers who'd lugged Chant into the house.

"Let him lay there till Pete Hawley shows up. You seen him today?"

"Nope. Reckon he's about due."

The cook studied Chant thoughtfully. "What if this jaybo ain't of a mind to wait around?"

"We'll take care of that," the man called Earl said. "Just lock the door on him."

Gabe scratched at his jaw. "Maybe we oughtn't to do that. He ain't done nothing but ride across Box C range."

The cook had caught onto the thought. "Maybe. If he's the one Curly was fighting with, that means he's the same woodchuck that was here in the yard snooping around. Now you catch him again . . . still snooping. I expect Pete'll want to ask why."

"Whyn't we just up and ask him?" Gabe suggested.

The cook leaned forward, shook Dave gently. "You hear me, mister? Who're you? What're you looking for around here?"

Chant, still playing it by ear, groaned deeply, remained silent.

The older man shook him again, this time with more insistence. "Talk up, dang it! Who are you?"

The question cleared up one thing in Dave Chant's mind—Curly and the two men with him that previous night had not known his identity when they jumped him. The attack, therefore, had been for no other reason than a grudge. He groaned again, rolled his eyes.

"He ain't going to say nothing," the cook said finally. "Just leave him for Pete. He'll get it out of him."

The men turned to the door. Gabe, his spirits higher, his voice more cheerful now that it appeared he might be some sort of hero after all, was recounting the facts of the shooting to the pair who'd met them in the yard.

"Reckon I sure done the right thing," he finished up.

Earl's tone was dry, sarcastic. "Maybe the boss'll give you a raise, you being such a high class gunslinger. Only after what that jasper done to Curly and Buck and Rufe, I don't want to be around when they turn him loose."

"Maybe they won't turn him loose," the cook said. "Leastwise, not if Wooton gets in on it."

XIV

Chant listened to the *click* of the door lock. It meant nothing. He could open it easily with the blade of his pocket knife if he elected not to wait around. He'd done it so many times as a boy. He sat up. The movement brought a grunt from his lips as pain rocked through his head. Gabe's bullet had rapped him harder than he'd thought.

He remained on the edge of the cot, hands to head for a long minute while the dizziness faded gradually. When it was over and the throbbing had subsided, he rose, stood in the center of the room, glancing about. It had been his father's quarters—and his mother's when she was alive. It was the largest bedroom in the house, and the new owners of Box C had converted it into a sort of bunk area for members of the crew. There were six cots, one against each wall and two in the center, he noted absently.

Crossing to the door, he placed an ear on the thin panel and listened. A low drone of voices came from the front of the house—from what had been the parlor. Pans were rattling in the kitchen, indicating that the cook had returned to his regular chores.

Coming about slowly, Dave re-crossed to the outside wall of the room, where a small window had been mounted. It was highly placed, but by standing on the cot he was able to look out into the yard. Recollection stirred within him; there were the garden, where they'd grown vegetables for the table, and the chicken yard—now both no more than weed patches surrounded by sagging, torn wire.

The trees in the small orchard Jared Chant had planted

appeared dead, and the peaked roof of the well house tipped low to one side where a support was missing. Farther on he could see the barn, the wagon shed, and various other buildings. All were in dire need of repair.

Disturbed, he resumed his seat on the cot. The Box C was in a state of decay—almost appeared to be falling down. Such could not have occurred in only two months. It would have taken a year, perhaps longer, of neglect for the place to become so dilapidated. That was odd! Jared Chant had been a strict man when it came to his holdings. Everything was cared for, repaired, replaced when necessary. What had changed his way of life—and when? Not that it mattered, particularly—Jared was dead, and the Box C was in the hands of outsiders. But Dave couldn't keep from wondering about it. With both Pa and Cliff on the premises it didn't stand to reason that all would go to hell as it apparently had.

Unless, of course, Jared Chant had just given up the fight. Cliff had mentioned a couple of bad winters, so severe, in fact, that the elder Chant had been compelled to borrow money in order to get by. That, combined with the probability that Cliff had not changed from his boyhood days and was still of little help around the place, could have broken the old man's spirit. Likely that was the answer. Cliff had never been much of a steady worker. He'd done his chores only because he was forced to. Dave had figured his brother would outgrow the failing with the years. He guessed he'd been wrong.

The sound of heavy footsteps in the hall reached Chant. His jaw tightened. He could be making a mistake hanging around, waiting, hoping to learn something that would be of help. The whole scheme could backfire now, especially if Con Wooton had his way. The gunman didn't like him, that was for sure.

The door rattled as someone tried the knob, then moved on—one of the riders checking the lock, assuring himself that all was well with the prisoner. Dave wished he was nearer the front of the house, where all the conversation was taking place. He could hear nothing from the bedroom. His thoughts came to a stop. There was a way to get closer. In the room he and Cliff had used they'd loosened two of the floorboards, fixed it so that at night, after Pa had turned in, they could slip out and do a little scouting around through the hills or maybe go for a swim in the river. The opening allowed them to drop down into the air space under the floor. An opening in the rock formation at its south end afforded an exit.

The room was down the hall, on the opposite side. The new owners could be using it for storage, or it might be Hawley's or Con Wooton's quarters. There was a chance the loose boards had been nailed down. Add to that the necessity for opening the door of the room in which he was imprisoned, entering the hall—it seemed the odds were all against him. But he was there in hopes of learning something about his father's killer, not just to sit back and wait for the Bar C foreman or Barr's gun hawk to show up and ask a lot of questions.

Reaching into his pocket, he found his knife and opened the largest blade. Moving to the door, he again crowded close to it and listened. He heard only the mutter of voices coming from the parlor, the sound of work going on in the kitchen. Slipping the blade between the lock's tongue and the notch in the facing, Chant pried gently. The iron wedge gave just as he'd known it would. Pulling on the knob carefully, he opened the door an inch and allowed the tongue to spring back into place without clicking. That done, he rose quickly and looked into the hall. All was clear.

Immediately he moved through the doorway, drew the panel shut, and allowed it to lock. He was pushing his luck a bit there, he knew. Should he be forced to return hurriedly, he'd have to use his knife on the lock again, and there could be a scarcity of time for it. He'd not even try, should it come down to that, he decided. He'd simply get out of the house, try to reach his horse, make a break for it.

He reached his old room in two long strides, tested the knob. It was not locked. The panel swung in, hinges squeaking faintly. Closing the door, he looked around. The room seemed hardly changed. The same two bunks built into the wall, the identical washstand with a cracked glass in a carved frame hanging above it, the same barrel and cowhide chairs. Someone was using the quarters, all right; he could see clothing hanging behind the curtain of the closet.

Wasting no more time, he crossed to the corner near the washstand. Taking the lightweight piece of furniture in his hands, he moved it a short distance to one side, reached for the corner of the rag carpet, laid it back. A half smile pulled at his lips. The boards had not been secured. Hurriedly he lifted the two planks. The opening was smaller than he remembered, but he could still get through. Scooting over, he lowered his legs, and then, crouched in the darkness beneath the house, he maneuvered one of the planks back into place, caught the carpet by the corner and drew it forward until it was propped up on the second board. A moment later he had worked it into position. He had performed the feat a hundred times in the past, and it had come easily. Anyone looking into the room would see nothing amiss other than the washstand having been shifted slightly to one side.

On hands and knees, he brushed at the cobwebs stringing across his face and made his way to a point where he was directly below the parlor. There was no sound of voices at the moment, and he had a quick wonder whether he'd figured wrong—perhaps he'd be unable to hear, after all. Then a distinct *click* reached him. He settled back. The men were at cards. Someone had just flipped a chip onto the pile.

"Up to you," a drawling voice said.

"Count me out." Gabe's tone was disconsolate.

"Me, too," someone else said, equally resigned.

"Where do you reckon Hawley is?" Gabe said after a pause. "I'm supposed to be out there on the south range."

"Then why ain't you?"

"Wanted to be here when Hawley come . . . tell him what happened."

"Expect we can do that for you," the drawling voice said.

"Lord knows you done told us about it often enough. Is he the first man you ever cut down?"

"First," Gabe admitted heavily. "Can't say as I admire the feeling."

"Man gets used to it. Doubt if a fellow like Wooton ever thinks twice about it after he's blasted some sucker."

"I ain't hankering to be no Con Wooton."

"Why not? He's making hisself plenty of money, running around doing what he's told. Sure beats nursing cows."

"Maybe not so healthy."

A chair scraped noisily against the floor. The man with the Texas drawl said: "When'd he get to be such a handy-andy with a hogleg? Ain't been too long ago he was chousing strays out of the breaks right alongside of me down in Arizona. Wasn't no fancy gun hand then. When'd he start working for this outfit?"

"Been a couple of months, maybe less. Sure must've caught on fast if what you're saying's true."

"It's for true. Oh, I seen him practicing some, now and then, twirling that prettied-up gun of his'n and seeing how quick he could pull it out of the leather. But that don't mean nothing. Just about every man I know does the same."

"Well, he got real good somehow." Chant recognized Earl's voice. "Barr wouldn't have hired him to do his leggin' if he wasn't. Don't think Con figures to hang around here much longer, howsomever. Was telling me he had a hankering for a place in Mexico. Aims to head down that way soon as he gets his stake."

Tex snorted. "At thirty a month and found it'll take a hell of a long time."

"Con makes a sight more'n that. Besides, he's already got hisself a fair-sized poke. Job he done for somebody, I think."

"He say how much?"

"Nope, and I weren't about to ask. Ain't smart to get nosey with him. But it must've been a good piece of change. Way he figures, he'll be able to pull out come next spring."

Dave stirred, easing his cramped muscles. All he'd learned so far was that Con Wooton was doing very well— so well, in fact, that he would be leaving the valley the next year. He brushed at the sweat on his face. It was hot under the house, and the heat would increase as the day wore on. But he didn't expect to remain there much longer. The men in the room above appeared to know very little. Twisting about, he looked to the end of the house for the opening in the foundation. It was there, overgrown with weeds, but still usable.

Someone above yawned loudly. A chair scraped once more. Boot heels thumped against the floor.

"Reckon we could promote the old man out of a cup of

Arbuckle's? Damned critters was restless last night. Didn't hardly get no sleep at all."

"Somebody coming."

"Hawley?" Gabe's voice was hopeful, anxious.

"Nope," Tex drawled. "Ain't him. It's Wooton."

XV

A door slammed. Heavy footfalls sounded on the porch, then in the parlor. Con Wooton's hard voice said: "Where's Hawley?"

"Ain't around," Tex replied in his lazy way. "Gabe here's been waiting for him."

"Shot me a trespasser," Gabe said, a note of pride now in his tone. "Some jasper that's been sort of hanging around. Figured Pete ought to maybe talk to him, see what he's after."

"What's his name?"

"Won't say. Can't get him to talk."

Chant again mopped at the sweat on his brow, straining to hear every word spoken.

"What's he look like?"

"Tall. Sort of empty eyes. Dark hair. Riding a sorrel."

The timbre of Con Wooton's voice changed. "Show me where he is," he said in a quick, expectant kind of way.

"In the bunkroom. Didn't want him getting loose. . . ."

The rest of Gabe's words were lost in a scraping of chairs and thudding of heels on the floor. Flat on his belly, Dave crawled hurriedly to the area beneath the bedroom floor.

"Thought you said you had him locked up in here?"

Wooton's voice was harsh, impatient. Chant caught the sound of men moving about, making a search.

"Was here. Locked that door myself . . . and it was still locked. You seen that."

"Couldn't have crawled out the window," Tex said. "Ain't even big enough for a kid."

There was a plaintive note in Gabe's voice. "I just can't figure how. . . ."

"Well, he sure ain't here," Wooton snapped. "Now, I'll tell you something. That bird's name is Chant. That mean anything to you jugheads?"

"Chant?" It sounded like the old cook to Dave. "He some relation to . . . ?"

"Son. Had two, seems. Been gone for quite a spell, but he grew up in this house. Likely knew some way of getting out."

"But there ain't no way!" Gabe protested.

"He ain't in here, is he? Now, I want that jasper. Every one of you get busy, go through this shack like you was hunting ticks on a dog. If you don't turn him up, go outside. Anybody look to see if his horse is still here?"

Someone crossed to the window, climbed onto the cot. "Standing right where we left him."

"Means he couldn't've got far. Start looking. I want that Chant . . . bad."

"Why?" Only Tex, it appeared, was not awed by Wooton.

"My business," the gunman snapped. "But since you're asking, he's been giving Mister Barr some trouble. Got my orders to handle it."

"What can he do to Mister Barr? Place was all foreclosed on legal-like, wasn't it?"

"It was. But this Chant ain't liking it much. Seems to think there was something crooked about the deal. Threatened to use a gun on Mister Barr."

Con Wooton lied easily, Dave thought. There had been neither suggestion nor promise of gun play in the merchant's office. Logically Wooton was also lying when he stated that Barr had given him orders to "handle it".

Elsewhere above, Chant could hear the other men tramping through the house, looking into the different rooms, poking about in closets and storage areas. If someone discovered the loose floorboards in the bedroom, he'd have to make a fast move for the opening in the foundation. But the corner went unnoticed. He listened while one of the riders moved through the room, and finally departed. No more conversation was taking place directly above him, and he guessed Wooton and Tex had rejoined the others, all gathering in the kitchen. There was no way to get beneath that part of the house. The quarters for the cook had been added onto the main building later, and the original foundation blocked the way.

Dave, crawling in as close as possible, struggled to hear, but there was only a low mumble of words. Most of the men would be in the yard anyway, pressing the search. Likely it was only Wooton and the cook.

It was steadily growing more uncomfortable under the house, where the air was trapped and stifling, but it would be foolish to leave now, with half a dozen men beating the brush in the yard for him. Best he stay now, stick it out and await developments.

Pulling himself around, he crawled a little nearer to the break in the foundation, where there was more air circulation, and stretched out full length. Once the search quieted down, he'd make his escape.

So far his efforts had proved of little value. He knew, of course, that Wooton hated him, probably because he posed a challenge to his position and would not hesitate to gain his end. But he'd learned nothing to strengthen the belief that his father had been deliberately murdered—that robbery had not been the primary motive.

Maybe he was wrong. It could all be as Harry Sloan and

Andrew Barr claimed. Even his own brother was accepting that explanation—and Cliff had been in on it from the start. Furthermore, what facts were available appeared to bear out their contention. Yet Dave Chant couldn't rid himself of the deep, disturbing hunch that all was not what it seemed. The feeling possessed him that all the answers were right there in the open for him to see—yet he couldn't, somehow, put his finger on them.

There had been more to the ambush than a simple fatal hold-up—a voice within him continued to tell him that. Yet he could turn up nothing that would strengthen the claim other than a few isolated incidents—being trailed by Wooton, old Heber's death, Harry Sloan's hostile attitude, Andrew Barr's refusal to discuss the matter at length, the reluctance of Aaron Faber and everyone else to talk. It all added up to nothing—could actually be explained away. All but Heber's death. That didn't fit. No one would have a reason to kill the harmless old man. He had been a threat to nobody, yet he had been mercilessly beaten to death—only a short time after he had talked from the shadowy protection of the shed. Dave mulled that over in his mind again. The pointless murder of the old swamper was the key to something—but to what?

Chant groaned, sleeved the sweat from his face. Maybe he'd best forget the whole thing, be on his way. Cliff was apparently satisfied, as much as he could ever be, and, crippled or not, he'd always have a home with the Gannons. Likely he didn't care one way or another whether he got the Box C back or not. Why, then, go on knocking his brains out trying to figure out something that possibly didn't exist at all? Jared Chant was dead. Nothing could change that, bring him back to life, and, if he'd been slain by some outlaw during the course of a hold-up, it was too late to do anything about that. After two months, the man could be a thousand miles away. Forget it. He'd already had one close call from a rifle bullet—next time he might not be so lucky. Move on . . . El Paso . . . Mexico. . . .

Chant awoke with a start. A curse slipped from his lips. He'd dozed off, and now it was near dark. He must have slept for hours in the hot confines beneath the house. He listened. No sounds were coming from the rooms above. Either the men were in the kitchen having the evening meal, or they were still outside. They would have given up the search for him by that hour, he was sure. They'd be mystified but convinced that he'd somehow got out of the house and escaped into the hills.

Twisting around, Dave worked his way to the opening in the rock foundation. Head close to the break, he lay for a brief time gulping in the cool, fresh air, and then quietly he drew himself into the opening.

Thick brush screened the hole in the rocks, and he could see only a small part of the yard. There could be men taking their ease close by, he knew, and realized he must depend upon his hearing rather than his vision in the next few minutes. For a time he remained there, ears cocked for the slightest sound. Over toward the barn someone was whistling tunelessly, but that was the only noise. Carefully he drew himself farther through the opening, using a clump of tough rabbit brush as a means for bracing himself.

It was not fully dark. The sun had gone, but afterglow filled the sky, covering the land with a pale gold cast. It would not hold for long, and he reckoned it best to wait for the moment when it would be gone. He settled back.

What next? Chant pondered that question. Give up, ride on, as common sense and all the signs indicated—or keep looking, keep searching, and try to satisfy that persistent inner voice which would not let him rest? It had to be that. He'd never have a minute's peace until he knew for sure. If the whole affair had been a scheme to get the Box C from his father and brother, then he must be convinced of it, take the necessary steps to set things right. If it was a case of robbery, as everyone wanted him to believe, then all well and good. He could then mount up and ride on, at peace with himself. But first he had to be certain.

The glow had faded. Darkness claimed the land, and long shadows now laid black strips and squares and irregular shapes upon the slopes and flats. The whistling near the barn had ceased, and a dull thudding of hoofs told of men riding out of the yard—the night crew heading out to assume their herd chores or the day crew riding into town for an evening of relaxation.

Chant heaved himself forward, thrust himself clear of the opening, lay quietly. He was in the shallow ditch that led away from the house to a sink some yards distant. It had been dug by Jared Chant years ago, and it served to drain off rainwater from the house. Both he and Cliff had made other use of it with their frequent truancies from bed. It would serve a like purpose now. Although much shallower due to accumulating wind-blown sand and rain-washed soil, it would still afford him a means for getting safely away from the corrals where he could expect to find his horse. But he'd manage that, too. By working his way through the neglected, weedy orchard, circling the lower corral, he'd. . . .

Chant's thoughts came to a stop as the sound of quiet footsteps reached him. He was a dozen paces from the protection of the house, and there was no returning. Holding his breath, he flattened himself in the trench. The steps moved by, continued briefly, halted near the tall brush to his left. Con Wooton's voice, low but distinct, came to him.

"You got something sticking in your craw?"

XVI

The reply was inaudible. Dave raised himself slightly and tried to see into the dense growth. Someone on a horse, evidently, but since he could make out nothing in the shadows, he could not be sure. One thing certain—whoever it was had taken pains to avoid being seen by others on the ranch.

"Had to." Wooton's voice was a harsh grumble. "Ain't sure how much blabbing he done."

The person in the brush made some remark.

Again the gunman's reply was gruff. "Was your idea."

There was that space of silence once more as words unheard by Chant were being spoken, and then came Con Wooton's reply, this time lifting with anger.

"To hell with that! I ain't ready . . . and nobody tells me what to do."

Dave swore silently in desperation. He was missing out on something that could be important—that could have a direct bearing on the problem he faced. Wooton's replies indicated it. He twisted his head, looked along the ditch. Perhaps if he moved forward, he might be afforded a view of the hidden person. Using care to make no sound, he began to inch his way down the ditch.

"Done just what you wanted," Con Wooton said in a brittle tone. "No fault of mine it ended up wrong for you."

Chant paused, wondering at the meaning of that remark. What had ended wrong? And for whom? Anxiously he resumed his slow forward progress. He must see who it was lurking in the dense clump of tamarisk. That was all he could do, he thought bitterly. With no weapon of any sort, he could do nothing but look—and listen.

"That's a god-damn lie!" Wooton snarled. "Nobody ever told me Barr was holding that note! Don't go saying I crossed you up!"

Chant had again come to a full stop. A mixture of satisfaction and anger was flowing through him. He had been right. There was something behind the murder of his father—something that related directly to Con Wooton and the man in the brush.

"Don't go losing no sleep over it. I'll take care of him." There was a quiet deadliness in the gunman's tone.

Take care of whom? Dave resumed his crawling with as much haste as he dared. The trench began to curve away from the windbreak. To follow it farther would lessen all the more the possibility of seeing the party with whom Wooton spoke. Chant glanced to his left. Open, grassy ground lay between him and the tamarisk. The moment he ventured onto it he would be in view of the gunman. Better off back the other way. If he could return to the house and cross behind Wooton, he could try working in from the opposite side. There were clumps of rabbit brush, groundsel, sage, all tall enough to offer him a screen.

"Forget it!" he heard Wooton snap. "You go spilling your guts and you're a dead man! Understand?"

Reversing himself in the shallow ditch, Dave began to retrace his course, using less caution, bent now on reaching a point where he could see the gunman's visitor before it was too late.

Halfway he drew up sharply, threw his glance to the side. The cook, a curved stem pipe clenched between his teeth, was standing no more than an arm's length away. A look of utter astonishment was on the older man's face.

"Hey!" he yelled, and then, wheeling, added: "Over here

. . . that drifter! He's right here!"

Wooton shouted something. The sound of his voice was followed by the quick hammer of hoofs. Chant threw a glance to the tamarisk, caught only the shadowy outlines of a dark horse with white stockinged legs racing off into the night. He wheeled then, and bolted past the cook, shouldering the man roughly into the side of the house.

Reaching the corner, he ducked low, and paused, aware of men running up from the rear of the building and other points in the yard in response to the cook's outcry.

"Where is he?"

That was Wooton. He reached the old man first.

"Jumped up, bee-lined it toward the corrals."

"Double back, some of you!" the gunman shouted. "He's trying to get his horse."

Dave, bent double, hurried along the pole-enclosed pen, the barn his objective. He'd never make it, he realized—not with men cutting in from the other side. They'd be between him and the larger structure.

Damn the luck anyway, he thought, ducking into the brush below the pens. He was onto something. In another couple of minutes he would have had all the answers he sought—and then he'd blundered into the cook, out taking his evening stroll. If he hadn't chosen to follow the ditch in the first place. . . .

"See him?"

Wooton was somewhere near the first corral. A voice answering from the yard said: "Ain't showed up here. You certain he headed this way?"

"Hell, yes, I'm sure. Would've had to climb over me if he went the other direction . . . or else up the side of the house."

"Maybe so, but he didn't come this way. Reckon he's

hiding inside one of the corrals?"

"Good chance. Couple of you fetch some lanterns."

Chant couldn't remain there. They'd spot him quickly. Keeping low, Chant eased out of the brush and, keeping close to the hedge of sage, worked his way in toward the barn. Maybe he could reach it without crossing open ground—but at the moment he could think of no way.

Boots pounded upon the hard pack. Lights began to bob along the corrals. Wooton's voice sounded. "Who's watching at the barn?"

"Amos and Dan Petrie. You want somebody else?"

"Just wanted to be sure we had him cut off."

Dave pulled back from the pens, glancing over his shoulder. No escape that way. Beyond the band of brush lay cleared country extending up a slope covered with short grass. His chances would be no better there than in the yard. But he had to do something. Slowly, surely, they were driving him toward the last corral. Beyond it he'd have no protection of any sort, and the barn, where at least two men waited, would still be a dozen long strides distant.

Double back—he could do nothing else—and hope to do so quietly and unseen and thus allow the searchers to by-pass him in the thick brush. They were intent upon ferreting out every corner of the string of pens. They just might overlook him.

He flattened himself in the sage, eyes on the moving splotches of yellow light marking the positions of the lanterns, drawing nearer. Shadows and dim outlines of figures took shape. Boots grated on gravel, wood squeaked as men climbing poles placed their weight upon the crossbars.

"Keep your eyes peeled!" Wooton warned. "Don't want him getting away again, or by God I'll. . . ."

Chant's attention swung to motion at the far end of the

pens, unrelated to the activity nearby. A rider had come into the yard and halted. Hope stirring within him, Dave watched the silhouetted man dismount and move toward the commotion among the corrals.

"What's going on?"

One of the men off the range or possibly one returning after a visit to town.

"Got that Chant bottled up here somewheres," a voice replied.

"He the one you had locked in the bunkroom?"

"Same. Come on over here, give us a hand."

The rider melted into the darkness off to the left. A moment later his voice sounded again. "Hey . . . you know old Heber, swamper at Kinsvater's? Somebody killed him."

"Heber?"

"Yeah. He was found in back of the place. Been beat up something terrible."

"They got any ideas who might've done it?"

"Marshal's saying maybe it was this here Chant fellow. Somebody claims he seen a stranger hanging around the back of the saloon. The way he described him, the marshal said it sounded like Chant."

"A dang' shame. Old Heber never hurt anybody. Why you reckon this Chant would do a thing like that?"

Flat on the ground, Dave swore softly. More bad luck. All he needed was for Harry Sloan to come barging in seeking to arrest him and get in the way just when he was onto something.

"Probably was Chant, all right," Con Wooton said from the darkness. "Let's roust him out of there. Be a good night for a little hanging."

The lanterns were drawing closer, and the grunts and an occasional curse were louder. There was motion ahead.

Con Wooton stepped into view, the tall crown of his hat scarring the dim wall of light behind him. If the gunman remained fixed, didn't move forward with the others. . . . Relief slipped through Chant. Wooton took a half a dozen strides deeper into the pens. Con had his pistol in hand, ready. Its silvered surface glinted now and then as light struck the flat places.

Abruptly Dave was behind the men. They'd worked past him, paid no attention to the clumps of weeds. Silently Chant wormed his way over the loose sand toward the horse left standing at the first gate. He reached that point and continued to lie quietly while he recovered his breath. He still had no weapon. Murmuring a prayer, he glanced to the saddle on the nearby horse. A rifle was in the boot. He grinned wryly. Maybe his luck was beginning to change for the better.

Reaching out, he seized the trailing reins, rose swiftly. The horse jerked away, startled by his sudden appearance, but he laid a firm grip on the leathers. Thrusting a foot into the stirrup, he swung to the saddle and whirled away, pointing straight for the band of tamarisk where Con Wooton's hidden friend had been.

At first *thud* of the horse's hoofs, a yell went up from the corral. Instantly a pistol shot cracked through the night shattering the stillness. Dave Chant didn't hear the bullet's passage. He guessed it had gone far wide. Luck again. In the next moment he was behind the tamarisk and racing on into the darkness.

XVII

The man on the dark horse—a black, Dave thought—would be well away from the area by this time, and there was no way of knowing in which direction he'd fled. Likely he had continued eastward for the settlement. Only ranches lay elsewhere—Gannon to the south, Arvie Klein beyond him, Corvallis on a narrow strip to the west, Jensen and a few others in the north.

Chamisa. He'd lay odds that was where he'd find the mysterious rider. Get to town as fast as possible, start a search for a dark horse with white stockings. Whoever the man was, he held the answer to all the questions that plagued Dave Chant's mind. The conversation he'd had with Con Wooton, although one-sided insofar as Dave was concerned, proved that. They'd been speaking of his father and the Box C, and doubtless Wooton's statement to the effect that he would take care of someone referred to Dave. Matters were coming to a head—and fast. He wanted to be ready. But first there was the little problem of getting Con Wooton and the half a dozen or more of his followers off his trail so that he could press the search for the man on the black horse. On a rise a quarter mile beyond the tamarisk windbreak, he drew to a halt and looked back.

In the pale glow of the moon he could see riders moving across the Box C's yard, rushing for the gate. It had taken them a few minutes to saddle up, but they were coming now. Spurring his borrowed horse off the roll, he rode south a short distance until he reached a broad, sandy arroyo thickly overgrown with greasewood and rabbit brush. The wash led back into a wild, eroded section of the land they'd called the breaks. Many times he'd been given the chore of working the tangled brush and numerous small side cañons for strays.

Turning into the arroyo, he pointed for a low line of bluffs a hundred yards or so immediately ahead. Gaining that, he cut left, found the trail he knew should be on the north side of the first formation, and climbed to a ledge halfway to the summit. From there he could watch the country below, see any pursuers who might also think of the breaks and the possibilities it offered for hiding.

They were not long in coming. No more than a quarter hour had elapsed when three riders appeared. Walking their horses slowly, they came up the arroyo abreast. Light from the moon was too weak to give them definition, but he was certain Con Wooton was not one of them.

He watched them approach the butte, halt, hold some sort of discussion. Shortly they split, two of the men circling the formation to its right, the remaining rider going left. They'd reunite on the east side of the butte and continue on.

Chant grinned into the darkness. They were looking for him on his own ground—a hopeless task. He knew every foot of the country, and, if he desired and had the time to spare, he could lead them on an endless game of hide-and-seek until their horses dropped. But he had more important things to do. Every minute that slipped by placed the man he sought that much farther away. He glanced to the east, wishing it was nearer daylight. He could then double back to the tamarisk windbreak, hunt around until he located the hoof prints of the black, determine exactly which direction the rider had taken.

Sunup, however, was hours away—and by doing so he

could be pressing his luck too hard. Doubtless Wooton would keep his men scouring the hills and flats, and he could encounter one or more of them. He didn't want to confront Con Wooton yet. Later, yes. When he was certain of what he suspected, he'd have a reckoning with the gunman.

Half turning, he listened into the night. The dry rattle and rustling of the three riders had faded as they worked deeper into the arroyo. Swinging his horse around, Chant descended the trail to the floor of the wash and headed back for the flat. By swinging farther south and cutting across country, he could avoid the usual route to town—also most likely being watched by Wooton's men. It would take an hour longer, but there was less risk of being stopped.

That small voice set up its cry within him again as he jogged steadily on. There was something he was over-looking, perhaps ignoring—something that would drop the pieces of the puzzle into place. He rubbed at his jaw impatiently, trying to bring whatever it was to the surface, but with no success. It was there, lying stubbornly in his mind, but he could not give it shape or meaning. Cursing himself, he pressed on. It would come to him . . . give it time.

He reached the mouth of the arroyo, halted momentarily to listen and assure himself there were no more riders waiting nearby, and then broke out onto the flat. He curved left, began to follow the outer fringe of the break. It would be growing daylight by the time he got to Chamisa, taking this roundabout trail. But he should reach there with no trouble. Few knew of the side route that crossed the hills at that point; the older ranchers, some of the cowpunchers who worked for them, had discovered the path when rounding up cattle. Newcomers would have no idea of its existence.

Abruptly he pulled to a halt. A man on a horse was standing no more than thirty paces away. A familiar figure—Con Wooton! Surprise rolled through Chant at finding the outlaw there. And then he remembered—Con had worked a time for Tom Gannon before lining up with Barr. It explained his knowledge of the trail and the hunch he undoubtedly had that the man he hunted would take it.

The gunman was slouched in his saddle, faced away. The soft sand had muted Dave's approach, and Wooton was unaware of anyone else's presence. Chant studied the man narrowly. There could be other riders close by. It could be a trap. Reaching forward, Dave pulled the rifle from its boot, doing it slowly, carefully, to avoid any creaking of leather. He'd feel much better with a six-gun in the holster at his hip, but they'd taken it from him back at the Box C.

Holding the weapon in his right hand, thumb on the hammer, forefinger on the trigger, he guided the horse to one side, drawing to a halt in a clump of brush. There he waited, listening. Wooton's horse stirred restlessly. The gunman straightened, glanced over his shoulder toward the flat, then resumed his vigilance of the trail. Con was alone. Chant became convinced of that. But he took no chances. Urging the borrowed horse forward, he walked the animal in a circle, eyes probing the undergrowth for other riders. None. Con Wooton had definitely chosen this trail as his personal trap.

Finally satisfied that it was a matter involving only the gunman and himself, Chant doubled over his own tracks and came in on Wooton from the left, thus putting the man's weapon on the far side.

Halting a short distance away, he said quietly: "Waiting to bushwhack me, Con?"

Wooton whirled on the saddle. Ignoring the rifle held by Dave, his hand flashed down, came up. Moonlight flickered off his pistol.

"God damn you!" he shouted. "I. . . ."

Dave triggered his weapon once, its blast blending with the sharper crack of the pistol. Wooton, jolted from the bullet's impact, sagged. The pistol slipped from his fingers, and he grabbed frantically for the horn as he fought to keep from falling while echoes rolled through the low hills.

Suddenly the gunman lost his grip and tumbled to the ground. Chant, dismounting, hurried to where the man lay. Kicking the gunman's silver-plated revolver beyond reach, he knelt beside him.

"Wooton . . . I know you killed my pa."

The gunman stared at him blankly through glazing eyes. "You . . . know . . . hell!"

Dave nodded. "No use denying it. What I want to know is . . . who hired you to do it?"

Wooton's mouth drooped. "Old bastard . . . tried to fight . . . me."

It had been a long shot, strengthened by what he had heard near the tamarisk break, but it had paid off. Wooton had murdered Jared Chant. But knowing that wasn't enough.

"Who hired you?"

Somewhere back of the flat, Dave could hear oncoming horses. Con's riders, hearing the gunshots, were moving in fast. He had to be ready for them.

"Wooton . . . speak up! Who hired you?"

The gunman's jaw sagged. He stared at Chant while a ragged smile pulled weakly at his lips.

"Go . . . to hell," he mumbled thickly, and went totally lax.

XVIII

Dave Chant looked down into the bleak features of the gunman, and then suddenly all became clear as the deeply buried thought in his mind broke through. He rose slowly, disbelievingly—but there it was, plainly, completely. Why hadn't he recognized it earlier? Why had it taken him so long to see it?

He started to turn, remembered the approaching riders. Throwing his glance to the flat, he made out four men. Cradling the rifle, he stepped over Wooton's body, taking up a position out of sight behind a squat cedar tree.

The men rushed in, halted. A lean-faced rider leaped from his saddle, hurried to Wooton, made a brief examination. Rising, he faced the others.

"Dead. That damned Chant. . . ."

"Was me, all right," Dave said, stepping into the open. "Had no choice. Wanted to talk, but he went for his gun."

The thin cowpuncher frowned. His glance touched the silver-plated pistol lying in the sand. He nodded.

"Expect that's the way it was. Con wasn't the listening kind."

They were all respecting the rifle held ready in his hands, Dave knew. He didn't want it that way, so he deliberately lowered the muzzle.

One of the men, still mounted, leaned forward, hands cupped on the saddle horn. "Mind telling us what the hell this was all about? All we know is that Con wanted us to run you down."

"He murdered my pa," Chant said. "Robbed him."

Someone whistled softly. A man with a Texas drawl said: "Reckon that's where he got that there stake he was taking to Mexico. Was about two thousand dollars, wasn't it?"

Chant nodded. "Close to that."

Another voice spoke up. "Old Heber . . . we heard maybe it was you who killed him."

"No, that was Wooton, too . . . leastwise, I'm pretty sure. I did some talking to Heber. He was an old friend of my pa's. He was beaten to death right after I left him. My guess is that he knew something Wooton didn't want passed on."

Tex turned his attention back to the gunman. "What'll we do with him?"

"I'd be obliged if you'll load him up, take him to town. Tell the marshal what happened and that I'll come in later . . . do my talking."

"Why don't you take him in yourself?" There was a thread of doubt in the rider's voice.

"Got another little chore to do. This thing's not over yet."

"That mean there's somebody else mixed up in all these killings?"

Dave nodded, lifting the rifle slightly. He was not too sure of these men. They were friends, after a fashion, of Con Wooton's, and he could afford to take no chances this late in the game.

"His horse is standing over there," he said, ducking his head at the gunman's bay, which had shied off into the brush after Wooton had tumbled from the saddle.

The lean-faced cowpuncher hesitated briefly, and then moved off, caught up the animal, and led him in close.

"While you're mentioning horses," a new voice said from the half circle edging the coulée, "mind doing some trading? That's mine you're forking . . . and I reckon this sorrel's yours."

Dave beckoned the man in. He glanced at the rider attempting to lift Wooton. "While you're on the ground, give your friend a hand," he said.

The gunman's body was finally aboard his horse, draped across the saddle. Chant watched the two men turn to their mounts.

"I'll be borrowing your rifle for a spell," he said to the one who'd been riding the sorrel. "I'll bring it back when I come for my pistol."

"Gabe's got it," someone offered.

"Tell him to leave it with the cook. I'll do the same with the rifle."

There was no response. The riders swung up, one catching up the reins of Wooton's gelding, and then they all moved off into the half light. Dave did not stir. He did not think it likely, but if any of them had ideas about taking him to face Harry Sloan before he was ready, he wanted to know it. But no such intention prevailed, and, when the last of the riders, still in a tight group, disappeared into the distance, Chant wheeled, went to the saddle, and, with the rifle resting across his legs, since he carried no boot, headed south for Gannon's.

He rode into the yard as first light spread its pearl flare in the east. Cold from the realization of what lay before him, half hoping he was wrong, he angled the red horse toward the barn. Pulling up to the rack, he dismounted slowly, looped the leathers over the rail, and then strode through the wide doors of the bulky structure into the runway. There were three stalls to his right, a horse in each. Other animals would be in the corrals, he knew, but they would be for use of the hired hands. The mounts favored by the family would be stabled separately.

Moving into the first stall, he laid his hand on the horse's rump—cold. He looked closer—not a black, and there were no white stockings. He continued to the second compartment, glanced first to the animal's legs—white. He touched the horse's withers—warm. A tautness claimed him as he reached into his pocket for a match. Gannon had been riding a black horse with white stockings when he encountered him on the range. That had been the nagging little thought, buried in his memory, that had plagued him. Striking the match, he reached for a lantern hanging from a peg at the end of the stall. A voice from the doorway checked him.

"Never mind," Tom Gannon said. "It was me. I knew you'd caught on when I saw you ride into the yard. I've been up all night, sweating this thing over."

Shaking out the match, Chant turned, thumb drawing back the hammer of the rifle. "I settled with Wooton," he said quietly. "Reckon you're next."

"Go ahead," Gannon said in a hopeless tone, lifting up his arms, then letting them drop. "It was all a big mistake . . . a hell of a mistake."

The rancher was unarmed. Dave lowered his weapon. "Mistake?" he echoed scornfully. "My pa's dead, my brother's a cripple, and you call it a mistake!"

"I mean the way it happened. You got to believe me, Dave. It wasn't supposed to end up the way it did. Things just got out of hand. Before God as my witness, I didn't figure on your pa getting killed . . . or even hurt!"

"That'll take some explaining."

"It was this way. I wanted to add the Box C to my spread. Always have . . . you know that."

"I remember," Chant said coldly.

"Things got bad for your pa. Real bad. He was running deeper into debt all the time, and the place was running down. . . ."

"Cliff was there."

"I know, but Cliff wasn't Jared . . . not like him at all. Just didn't have the knack of running a ranch, doing things right. Long as his pa was on him, telling him, he could do a passable job. Otherwise, everything was always wrong. Jared, I reckon, finally gave up on him, and the place mighty quick showed it. I made an offer to buy then, but you know your pa. He wouldn't listen to me. He had a lot of pride, being as he was the first man to settle this valley. But that didn't count for much when it came to keeping a ranch going, on its feet."

"So you had him murdered, hired Con Wooton to do it for you."

"No . . . no! Not that way at all. Leastways, it wasn't supposed to end in killing. I knew about Jared's owing the bank and that he'd raised enough cash to pay off, save the place from being foreclosed on. Got an idea . . . a wrong one, maybe, but I meant well, Dave, you got to believe that, too. How I could help Jared, and have what I'd always wanted."

"The Box C."

"That's it. I figured if Jared didn't make that payment, Aaron Faber and the bank would take the ranch over. Then I'd step in, pay off the note, and the place would be mine."

"The bank didn't hold the note."

"That's what I didn't know. When I went in to make the offer to Faber, he told me Andrew Barr had bought up the note, and Barr wasn't interested in selling the ranch except at full value."

"So you got Pa killed for nothing," Chant said in his cold, flat way. "You pulled the trigger the same as Wooton did."

"That wasn't the deal I had with Wooton. I told him about Jared going to take the money in to the bank, put the idea in his mind to pull a hold-up so's your pa wouldn't be able to meet the note. That's all it was supposed to be . . . a hold-up."

"But Con lost his head or something, killed Pa?"

"That's just what happened. I didn't intend for it to end that way, so help me! I jumped Wooton after it was all over. He laughed at me. He said he'd handled it to suit himself, not me. If it'd worked out right, I had in mind to take Jared in, have him make a home right here with me. He'd never want for anything . . . and he'd never have to work another day in his life."

Chant shrugged. "You're fooling yourself, Tom. Pa'd never take your charity."

"Well, I thought. . . ."

"You figured wrong from the moment you got the idea," Dave cut in harshly. "Trying to get your hands on the Box C that way was your first mistake. Trusting a man like Con Wooton was the second. And thinking Pa would mooch off you the rest of his life was the third. He'd have died first."

Tom Gannon stared at the littered floor of the stable. "I realize all that now, but I wasn't seeing it that way at the start. I don't know what I ought to do next."

"I ought to kill you," Chant said. "Maybe that would make up a little for Pa . . . and for old Heber. But I'm not much in favor of this eye for an eye business. I use a gun when I have to, sure, but this. . . ."

The rancher shook his head. "I wouldn't blame you if you did. How am I going to explain all this to Sarah

. . . and Cliff? I don't know."

"It's your problem," Dave said curtly. "You're the man who turned the dogs loose."

Gannon raised his troubled eyes to Chant. "What about you?"

"I'm heading back to town, square myself with the marshal . . . and tell him all you've told me."

"I'll ride in with you."

Dave pointed to the house. "No, there're two people in there you'd better start putting yourself right with first," he said, and walked on to where the sorrel waited.

"It's up to you," Dave Chant said. "The ranch is yours, if you want it back. I told Barr the way it was, and he said he didn't want to let the foreclosure stand under those conditions. He'll rewrite the note, give you time to get things going, pay off the note. I figured he'd see it that way."

Cliff, propped by pillows on the bed, smiled, reached out his hand. "No way of telling you my thanks. Hadn't been for your coming by. . . ."

"Forget it. You've got a big reason to climb out of that bed now. You've got something . . . and somebody . . . to work for."

"I'll make it," Cliff said, smiling at Sarah. "Can't miss. And if things don't go right, I can join up with Tom, make the Box C and the Triple X one big spread."

Sarah turned to Dave. "I want to thank you, too. For what you've done for Papa . . . what you said."

"Only the truth," Chant said, shrugging. "Down deep I reckon he was doing what he figured was a good thing. Where does it stand now?"

"Marshal Sloan said he'd wait until the circuit judge came, put the matter before him. He doesn't think there'll

234

be any charges. He thinks, too, that Papa's been punished enough by his own feeling of guilt."

"I expect the marshal's right. Tom'll be facing that every time he looks into a mirror. Well, I've got to be moving out. Sloan wants me out of the country by dark."

"He give you any trouble?" Cliff asked.

"Not 'specially. Just made it plain I wasn't welcome in these parts. Clearing up this mess didn't change his opinion of me much, it seems."

"The devil with him! Stay on, Dave. Help Sarah and me put the ranch back together. We could. . . ."

Cliff's words faded as Dave Chant began to shake his head.

"I'm obliged to you for the offer, but I wasn't cut out to nurse cows. Anyway, I'll be dropping in again. I want to see the Box C fixed up and going strong when I do."

"You will," Cliff said. "So long."

Dave Chant moved out onto the porch. Sarah pulled the panel closed, laid her hand on his arm, brought him to a halt.

"Dave . . . I. . . ."

"It's all right," he said, cutting off the words he knew she was striving to voice. "Say . . . I almost forgot. I brought a wedding present for you and Cliff. I got it for Pa, but now I figure you ought to have it."

Stepping to the sorrel, he unbuckled his saddlebags and procured the small, well-wrapped parcel. "A barometer," he said. "It'd be nice to hang on your wall, let you know when bad weather's blowing in . . . and maybe make you re-member me."

Sarah stepped up close. Eyes soft, she kissed him on the cheek. "I'll need nothing to remember you by, Dave Chant."

He grinned at her as he swung onto the saddle. "Good for a man to know he won't be forgotten," he said, and rode out of the yard.

About the Author

Ray Hogan was an author who inspired a loyal following over the years since he published his first Western novel, EX-MARSHAL, in 1956. Hogan was born in Willow Springs, Missouri, where his father was town marshal. At five the Hogan family moved to Albuquerque where they lived in the foothills of the Sandia and Manzano mountains. His father was on the Albuquerque police force and, in later years, owned the Overland Hotel. It was while listening to his father and other old-timers tell tales from the past that Ray was inspired to recast these tales in fiction. From the beginning he did exhaustive research into the history and the people of the Old West, and the walls of his study were lined with various firearms, spurs, pictures, books, and memorabilia, about all of which he could talk in dramatic detail. "I've attempted to capture the courage and bravery of those men and women that lived out West and the dangers and problems they had to overcome," Hogan once remarked. If his lawmen protagonists seem sometimes larger than life, it is because they are men of integrity, heroes who through grit of character and common sense are able to overcome the obstacles they encounter despite often overwhelming odds. This same grit of character can also be found in Hogan's heroines, and in THE VENGEANCE OF FORTUNA WEST (1983) Hogan wrote a gripping and totally believable account of a woman who takes up the badge and tracks the men who killed her lawman husband by ambush. No less intriguing in her way is Nellie Dupray, convicted of rustling in THE GLORY TRAIL (1978). One of his most popular books, dealing with an earlier period in the West with Kit Carson as its protagonist, is SOLDIER IN BUCKSKIN (Five Star Westerns, 1996). Above all, what is most impressive about Hogan's Western novels is the consistent quality with which each is crafted, the compelling depth of his characters, and his ability to juxtapose the complexities of human conflict into narratives always as intensely interesting as they are emotionally involving. TRUTH AT GUNPOINT will be his next **Five Star Western**.

The employees of Five Star hope you have enjoyed this book. All our books are made to last. Other Five Star books are available at your library, through selected bookstores, or directly from us.

For information about titles, please call:

(800) 223-1244

or visit our Web site at:

www.gale.com/fivestar

To share your comments, please write:

Publisher
Five Star
295 Kennedy Memorial Drive
Waterville, ME   04901